THE CHILD'S BOOK OF NATURE:
AIR, WATER, HEAT, LIGHT, ETC.

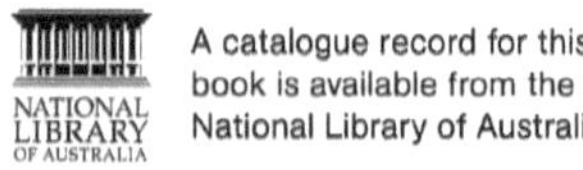
NATIONAL
LIBRARY
OF AUSTRALIA
A catalogue record for this
book is available from the
National Library of Australia

The Child's Book of Nature:
Air, Water, Heat, Light, etc.

WORTHINGTON HOOKER

CONTENTS

PREFACE.

THERE IS no obvious connection between the subjects now to be considered and those which were presented in Parts First and Second. But, after looking at what is of interest in the plants and animals that live in air and water, it seems appropriate to pass to the examination of the phenomena that air and water themselves furnish to us. And then with these subjects are naturally associated the other subjects contained in this Part—light, heat, electricity, etc.

Let me not be understood to say that the subjects treated in this Part are entirely disconnected from those in the other two Parts. There are many points of connection, resulting from the dependence of life upon air, water, heat, etc., and also from the mechanical principles that are brought into operation in the living machinery of both plants and animals. Still, the connection is not of that obvious and intimate character which we see between the subjects of Parts First and Second.

I have placed these subjects last in the Child's Book of Nature because they are not, for the most part, so easily understood as the subjects contained in the other Parts. The mind of the learner needs the training in observation and reasoning which it has in studying the phenomena of plants and animals to enable it to grasp all of the points which are here presented; and as in matter, so in style, I have supposed an advance of mental power in the learner. I have relaxed a little my strictness in simplicity. Indeed, I did so in a small degree in the Second Part. I have been careful, however, not to allow myself too much latitude in this respect, but have endeavored throughout to make the advance both in style and matter to correspond with the advance of mental capacity in the learner, and not go beyond it.

The subjects of this Part are those which are commonly ranged under the general term Natural Philosophy. They are not presented either formally or fully, but those points are selected which will interest a young beginner and be intelligible to him. I have made it an object to exclude all that are of a different character, for it is very important that the young learner should not be discouraged with difficulties and burdened with uninteresting matters at the outset.

It will be seen, however, that in making the selection alluded to, I have, after all, given quite a full view of the fundamental parts of the different subjects. The simple principles which form the basis of Natural Philosophy are most of them very fully illustrated. And I can not forbear remarking that many older scholars, who have pursued the study in the more formal manner common in our schools, might find their ideas rendered more clear and definite by looking at the simple views here presented.

I would call the attention of the teacher to one feature in my mode of developing scientific subjects to the young, which I deem to be of great importance. I observe a natural gradation in their development, beginning with the sim-plest views, and leading the learner gradually to those that are more complex and less easily understood. Not only is one thing given at a time, but each thing is put in its right place. I will cite a single example. Take what is said about air. First, the simple and single fact that it is a material thing is illustrated. This is followed by noticing what it does when in motion. Then I show how, by its resistance, birds and insects rise on the wing. Next I pass to the pressure of the air, first illustrating, in a simple way, the fact of its pressure in all directions, and then passing to show how its pressure operates in the pump and in the barometer. Then come illustrations of its pressure as exhibited in experiments with the air-pump, the immense pressure which the body sustains from it, and the manner in which it does this being especially noticed and explained. Next follows the elasticity of the air when compressed, illustrated by the operation of pop-guns, air-guns, etc. Then is illustrated the pressure of the air in making balloons, bubbles, and other light things rise in it. This leads naturally to the consideration of the rising of smoke and the operation of chimneys. And then, lastly, in the latter part of the book, the action of the attraction of gravitation upon the air is noticed, thus ultimately arriving at the real cause of most of the phenomena of the air's pressure.

Another feature, to which I will barely allude, is a frequent reference to analogies. Thus, for example, in giving the facts about air, I point out the resemblance between flying and swimming, between the action of compressed air and that of compressed steam, and of the gases produced by burning powder, etc. This feature not only adds interest to the various subjects, but makes the points in hand more clear, and gives a wider range to the views of the learner.

It is the author's intention to follow this with other books calculated to carry forward the scholar in his observation of nature. Indeed, I have already published two books, "First Book in Physiology" and "Human Physiology," by which the scholar can proceed with the study of the subjects treated of in Part Second of this book; and as soon as I can do so, I shall write some books for the purpose of enabling him to go on with the study of the subjects treated of in the other Parts. The whole together will constitute to some extent a series of books on the sciences, adapted to the different degrees of advancement in the pupils.

It will be observed that in this Part there are many experiments spoken of. These the teacher should try before the pupils so far as is practicable. I have also made extensive use of common phenomena as illustrations of the points presented. This will tend to form in the scholar the habit of observing what is just around him—the common things, so much overlooked in education—a habit which is a never-failing source of information and enjoyment. And both teacher and scholar, if they catch the spirit which I have endeavored to infuse into the book, will from their own observation add to the illustrations that I have given, and thus materially increase the interest of the daily recitations.

WORTHINGTON HOOKER.

CHAPTER I.

AIR.

WE SPEAK of a room having no furniture in it as being empty; but this is not exactly so. There is one thing that it is full of up to its very top. It is a thing that you can not see; but it is as really a thing as the furniture that you can both see and feel. This thing is air.

If you take all your books out of a box in which you keep them, you think of the box as having nothing in it; but it is full of air; and when you shut it up and put it away, you put away a box full of air. When the books were in it, it was full of books and air together; but now it is full of air alone.

You see some boys playing foot-ball. What is it that they are kicking about? It is an India-rubber ball, you will say. But is this all? Is there not something else besides the India-rubber? Suppose that you prick a hole in the ball. It is good for nothing now; but the India-rubber is all there. What makes it good for nothing? It is because the air escapes from the hole. The ball is of no use unless you can keep it full of that thing that we call air; and in playing with it, you kick about air locked up in the India-rubber.

You have heard of life-preservers, and perhaps you have seen them. They are India-rubber bags that you can fill with air by blowing into them. They are made of such a shape that they can be tied around the body. When used in this way, a life-preserver will keep one from sinking in water. But why? It is the air in it that does this. The air is as really a thing as the water is, but it is a lighter thing, and therefore a thing full of air will float on the water. If you kick a foot-ball into the water, it will float, because it is full of that light thing—air. But if you should prick a hole in it, and press out the air, and then throw it into the water, it would sink. So, too, the life-preserver would do no good if you tie it around you without blowing it up. It is the air that you blow into it that buoys you up in the water.

Why does a boat float on the water? It is not because the boat itself is lighter than the water is. It is commonly heavier, because there is so much iron about it. The reason that it floats is that it is full of air. Even a boat made entirely of iron will float for the same reason. But if there should be a leak, so that the boat can be filled with water, it will sink. So, too, it will sink if you put too much weight in it.

You have heard of life-boats. These are made in such a way that they will not sink, even if they are filled with water. How do you think that they are made to be so much lighter than other boats? It is not because they are built of different materials. They are made of wood, and are fastened together in every part with iron. Sometimes they are made entirely of iron. But they are built in a different way from common boats. They are made double, and in such a way that there are chambers of air between the two parts. These chambers are air-tight. If they were not they would do no good. If there were any opening into these chambers, the water would go in and force out the air. The boat would no longer be a life-boat. It would be of no more use than a life-preserver with no air in it, or with water instead of air.

You can not see air, although it is a thing; but you can sometimes feel it. You can not feel it while it is still, as you can such things as a table or water. You can only feel it when it is in motion. When the wind blows upon you, it is air in motion that you feel. When there is a gust of wind, as we say, the air comes against you just as a wave of water does. When you fan yourself, you make the air strike upon your face, and you feel it as you feel any thing else that strikes you, as water or a stick.

The air is transparent, or clear, like glass; that is, it lets the light come through it to your eyes. Sometimes glass is not clear, and you can not see things plainly through it. So, also, the air is sometimes not clear, as when there is dust flying in it, or when there is a fog.

Though you can not see air, you can see what it does when it is in motion. You can see it move the trees and other things. This I will tell you about in the next chapter.

The air is a thing which is necessary to our life. If it be shut out in any way from our lungs, great distress is immediately produced; and if it be shut out only for a few minutes, death occurs. I have told you in Part II., in the chapter on breathing, why it is that breathing air is so necessary to life.

Air is as necessary to the life of plants as it is to the life of animals. In animals the air is used by lungs, but in plants it is used by the leaves. This I have told you about in the chapter on the uses of leaves, in Part I.

Air is needed for another thing. Nothing can burn without air. It is the air that makes wood, and coal, and oil, and gas burn when fire is put to them.

The air that is all around the earth does not reach to the sun, and moon, and stars. It extends about forty-five miles above the earth. Beyond this there is no air. You will want to know how this was found out, as no one has ever been so far from the earth. I will not explain this to you now, for you are not old enough to understand it.

Questions.—What is a room full of when the furniture is all taken out? Tell about the box of books and about the foot-ball. What is said about life-preservers? Why does a boat float on the water? How are life-boats made? Can you see air? Can you feel it when it is still? What is wind? What is said about the transparency of air? What is said about its being necessary to the life of animals? What about its being necessary to the life of plants? What else is air needed for? How high does the air extend?

CHAPTER II.

AIR IN MOTION.

THE AIR, when it is in motion, does a great deal of work for us. It pushes along the ships in the water. Perhaps you think that it hardly sounds right to say that the air pushes the ships; but it really does push them. The sails are large, broad handles for the air to press against in pushing the vessels along in the water. On this page is a ship with many sails, and most of them are unfurled, or put out for the breeze to press upon.

The air would push a vessel along to some extent, even if there were no sails, by pressing or blowing against the

body of the vessel; but, unless the wind blew very strong, the air would not push it along very fast in this way. And so sails are put up on masts, that more of the air may get hold, as we may say, so as to press on the vessel.

Sometimes the wind helps you along as you are walking. Now, if you take hold of your coat, and spread it out wide, as you see this boy is doing, it will be like a sail, and the wind will carry you along faster, because there is more for the air to press upon. So, too, if you have an umbrella open when the wind is blowing on your back, it will be to you as the sail is to the ship. But if you are going against the wind, the outspread coat and the open umbrella would prevent your getting along fast.

When a tree is bare, the wind scarcely moves its branches; but how it bends when it is full of leaves and the wind blows strongly upon it! It is then like a ship with its sails all unfurled; there is a great deal for the air to press upon.

Sometimes we say the wind blows very hard or very strong; this is when the air moves very fast. The faster it moves, the more it will do. This is so with other things. When you strike any thing very hard with a stick, you do it by making the stick move fast. When there is only a gentle breeze, that you can just feel, the air is moving very slowly; it is like the gentle touch with the stick. But when the wind blows so hard that you can scarcely stand up, the air is moving very fast.

If a bullet is tossed to you, it will not hurt you to catch it, because it does not move very fast; but if a bullet shot from a gun should hit your hand, it would wound it, and perhaps go through it. The reason is, that the bullet moves so fast. The faster it moves, the more harm it will do. So the air, when it moves very fast indeed, is apt, like the bullet, to do harm.

You have seen a locomotive backed up against a train of cars to be hitched on. It does no damage, because it is backed up slowly. It only gives a little jerk, you know, to the whole train. Now, if it moved very fast, it would, when it came to the cars, break them to pieces. It is for the same reason that fast-moving air roots up trees, blows down houses, and drives ships on shore, dashing them against the rocks.

When the wind blows hard, the sailor takes in some of his sails. The vessel would go too fast if he left them all out, because there would be so much for the air to press on. If the wind blows very hard indeed, he takes down all the sails, fastening them very tightly, so that the wind may not loosen them. Even with all the sails down the ship will go quite fast enough, perhaps even too fast, pushed along by the wind that strikes right upon it. Here is a ship in a storm. You see how the sailors have tied up most of the sails. One of them has been torn from its fastenings by the violence of the wind, and is in tatters.

The waves that you sometimes see rise so high are made by the striking of the air upon the water; and the faster the air moves over the water, the higher they rise. When the air is very still there is scarcely a ripple, and the water

A COAT USED AS A SAIL.

looks like smooth glass; and you would hardly think, as you look upon it, that such a light thing as air is could whip it into such waves as you sometimes see.

The waves in the ocean are much higher than they are in a river. This is because the wind blows over so much greater an extent of water in the ocean.

You have heard of whirlwinds. In these the air moves in a whirling way instead of straight forward. You sometimes see little whirlwinds in the street; and as shavings and other light things are whirled about in them, and are carried up in the air, you can imagine what damage large whirlwinds can do, twisting up trees and tearing houses in pieces.

As you can not see the air, and it is a very light thing, you commonly think of it as being almost nothing, and yet it does these great things that I have mentioned. When we see this light thing raise the waves, and move the heavy ships along so swiftly, we see that there is great power in it.

Questions.—*How* does the air make a ship go? What is the need of sails? What is said about the air's helping you along in walking? Why does the wind bend a tree so much that is covered with leaves? What is true about the air when the wind blows hard? Give the comparison about the stick, the bullet, and the locomotive. Why does the sailor take down some of his sails when the wind blows hard? What is said about waves? Why are they higher in an ocean than in a river? What is said about whirlwinds?

CHAPTER III.

FLYING AND SWIMMING.

YOU CAN jump off from the ground just a little way into the air, but you can not fly into it, as the birds do. It is because you have no wings. But how is it that the birds fly with their wings? They push themselves up with them into the air. But perhaps you will say that they do not have any thing to push against, for there is nothing but air about them. Now it is the air itself that they push against. They press down upon the air with their wings, just as you press with your feet on the ground when you jump up; and as the bird, when it gets once started, keeps working its wings, it goes up and up, pushing down against the air each time that its wings are moved.

It is necessary that birds should have very large wings to raise themselves up thus in the air. If their wings were small, they would do no good, because they would not press upon enough of the air. You can move your hands in the same way that the bird does its wings, but you can not raise yourself off from the ground. Why? Because your hands are so small that they press only upon a little of the air. If your hands were as broad for you as the wings of birds are for them, and you had the proper muscles to work them, you could fly.

You can learn to fly, but it is in the water, and not in the air, that you can do it. Swimming is really flying in water. The hands and feet do for the swimmer what the wings do for the bird. He presses against the water with his hands and feet in the same way that the bird does against

THE TAIL OF A FISH LIKE A SCULLING OAR.

the air with its wings. Sometimes you see a bird dive down from a great way up in the air, in the same way that the swimmer does in the water. When it does this its wings are very still, and are folded close to its side, as you see here in the kite; but when it goes up again it works its wings up and down, just as the swimmer works his feet and hands when he is rising in the water.

Fishes swim chiefly with their tails. The tail is to a fish in the water what wings are to a bird in the air. It acts like a sculling oar in a boat, as I told you in Part Second, Chapter XXIII. The fins are the balancers, while the tail works the fish forward by its quick movements to one side and the other. You can see this very plainly if you watch gold-fishes as you see them in a glass vessel.

Observe why it is that you can not fly with your hands in the air in the same way that you can swim with them in the water. The water gives way under your hands just as the air does, but the air gives way much more easily than the water, because it is so much lighter. As the air gets out of the way so easily, you can not fly in it unless you have something very broad, so as to press down on a great deal of it at the same time. To fly, you must have large wings instead of small hands.

You can see what a difference there is between hands and wings by trying a little experiment. Move about your hand in the air. You do it with perfect ease, and the air does not seem to resist the hand at all. Now take a large palm-leaf fan and move that about. You can not do this so easily as you moved your hand, unless you move it edge-wise. Why is this? Because it presses upon so much more air than your hand does, and the resistance of so much air to the fan you can feel as you push it out of the way. The fan takes hold, as we may say, of more air than your hand does, and so does also the wing of a bird.

Did you ever think how large wings you would need to fly with? You would have to press upon a great deal of air to carry your body up as the birds do theirs. See how large the wings of a bird are, as they are stretched out. They are both very long and very broad; and, besides, the bird is not so large as he seems to be. You will see this if all the feathers are stripped from its body. If this be done while the wings are left whole, it will seem to you that it takes very large wings to raise a very little body. You can see, then, that it would require very large wings indeed to carry your body up in the air; and still larger ones to carry up a man.

Here is a bird that flies so fast that it is called the swift. Its wings, you

WINGS OF THE SWIFT.

see, are very long. You do not see how broad they are, because they are not fully spread out in the figure.

But there is no animal that has a greater extent of wing than the bat, unless it be

some of the insects. This is the reason why it flies so swiftly. You can see in this figure of the long-eared bat what a large amount of air its wings press upon as it works them. The wings of insects that fly very swiftly are very large in proportion to their bodies. This you can see in the butterfly that flies so nimbly from flower to flower. Those that fly rather slowly, as the bumble-bee, have not very large wings.

I believe that there is only one kind of fish that can fly in the air. It is represented here.

THE FLYING FISH.

You can see that the fins with which it flies are not nearly so large as the wings of a bird of the same size would be. It therefore can not fly very high or far. The highest that it was ever known to fly is twenty feet, and usually it skims along only two or three feet above the water. It does not go up into the air in the same way that a bird does. It gets

THE FLYING SQUIRREL.

its upward start from the water, and all that it does with its wing-like fins is to keep itself up, which it sometimes does for perhaps five or six hundred feet. It takes this flight in the air in fleeing from some large fish, and in this way often escapes being devoured.

That beautiful animal, the flying squirrel, which you see here, has a fold of skin extending from the fore leg to the hind leg on each side. These folds answer somewhat as wings when they are stretched out. Very graceful is the movement when the animal takes a long, flying sweep from one tree to another. But he can not go up in the air as a bird does, for the folds are not nearly so large as real wings, and so do not press upon enough air to carry him up. He can only take the sweep that I have mentioned.

Observe the shape of the wings of birds. They are rather rounded on the upper surface, and hollowed out underneath. They are shaped in this way to make the flying easy. This I will explain to you. When raising the wing, the air goes easily off from the rounded surface; but when it is moved downward, the air can not get away easily from the hollowed surface. The wing gets hold, as we may say, of some of the air, and, pressing upon it, raises up the bird.

You can see how this is by moving an open umbrella in the air. You can move it very easily if you push the outer rounded surface straight forward against the air. This is because the air moves off from the round surface of the umbrella as easily as it does from the upper surface of the bird's wing. But if you move the umbrella with the inner hollowed surface against the air, you find it rather hard work. Why? It is because the air is caught in the hollow of the umbrella as it is in the hollow of the bird's wing.

But this is not all. The bird, in raising its wing, does not move it straight upward. It moves it in such a way that it rather cuts the air with its forward edge. It does this to get it up with little resistance from the air. But when it moves it downward, it wants to get as much resistance from the air as it can, so it moves it straight down, and not edgewise. You can see how this works by moving a palm-leaf fan about in the air. Move it edgewise, and it goes very easily. This is like the upward motion of the bird's wing. But move it broadside against the air, and you feel considerable resistance. That is, the air resists the pressure of the fan, just as it resists the pressure of the wing in the downward stroke.

The swimmer manages his hands in the water in the same way that the bird does its wings in the air. When he raises his hands forward, he does it edgewise; but when he presses them down, he moves them flat against the water, so as to press upon as much water as he can.

Questions.—How is it that birds fly? Why do they have large wings? Why can you not fly? How is swimming like flying? What do fishes swim with? Why can not you fly in the air as well as swim in the water? Tell about the experiment with the fan. What is said about the size of birds' wings? Tell about the bird called the swift. Tell about the bat. What is said about the flying fish? What about the flying squirrel? What is said of the shape of wings of birds? Give the comparison of the umbrella. Tell how the bird moves its wings upward and downward. Give the comparison of the fan. Give the comparison about swimming.

CHAPTER IV.
THE PRESSURE OF THE AIR.

THE AIR is every where. It is always ready to go where there is room made for it. If we move a bureau or any thing out of a room, the air fills up all the place where it stood. If you make a hole in any thing, the air at once presses in to fill it up. Every crack and crevice is filled with air.

You know how much water a sponge will hold. There are a great many little cells or spaces in it that hold the water. Now squeeze the water out, and as the water goes out of these cells, the air presses into them and fills them up. So, too, if you have any liquid in a barrel, just so fast as you draw it off, the air goes in to take its place.

When you pull the handles of a pair of bellows apart, as represented here, you make more space in the bellows, and the air rushes in to fill up this space. It is the same with breathing. When you breathe in, or draw a breath, as we say, the air goes down into your lungs through the windpipe. This is because the chest is made larger as it heaves, and so

there is more room in the lungs; and the air goes in to fill up this room, just as it does in the bellows.

When the air moves very fast, it is, you know, often very inconvenient, and sometimes does much harm, as when houses are blown down, or when ships are driven upon a rocky shore. But commonly it is very accommodating. It is so easily moved out of the way that we do not think of its being in the way at all. When you are walking, your body pushes the air one way and the other, just as a man pushes persons to the one side and the other when he goes through a crowd; and as the people close up behind him as he moves along, so the air closes up behind you as you walk through it. Now, if the crowd were facing him, and should push against him, he would find it slow and hard work to get through. So, when the wind blows strongly in your face, it is hard walking, and you get along slowly, because the air presses against you so hard.

The air is pushed out of the way easily because it is so light. This is the reason that it is easier to walk in air than in water. The water, as you wade in it, is pushed to the one side and the other, as the air is when you walk in it; but it is not done so quickly and easily; and, as it is easier to walk with the wind than against it, so it is easier, in a running stream, to wade down stream than up against the current.

The air is so light a thing that you hardly think of it as pressing on any thing; but it does press on every thing. Let us see what this pressure does.

See this glass tube. It is open at the end which is in the vessel of water, but it is closed at the other end. It is full of water. But water is apt to run down whenever it can get a chance to do it. Now what makes it stay up in this tube? It is kept up by the air that presses on the water in

the vessel. If you could take away the air from all about the vessel, the water in the tube would come down into the vessel, because there would be nothing there to hold it up.

There is another way in which the water in the tube can be made to run down into the vessel. Let a little hole be made in the top of the tube, and the air will go into it, and make the water run down by pressing on it. Even if it be only a pin-hole, the air, ready to go in every where, will rush in, and down the water will all go. Now you can not very well make a hole in the top of the tube, but you can try the experiment in another way, so as to show what letting the air in will do. The experiment is represented here. You take a glass tube open at both ends. Covering one end tight with the palm of your hand, you fill the tube with water. Then carefully

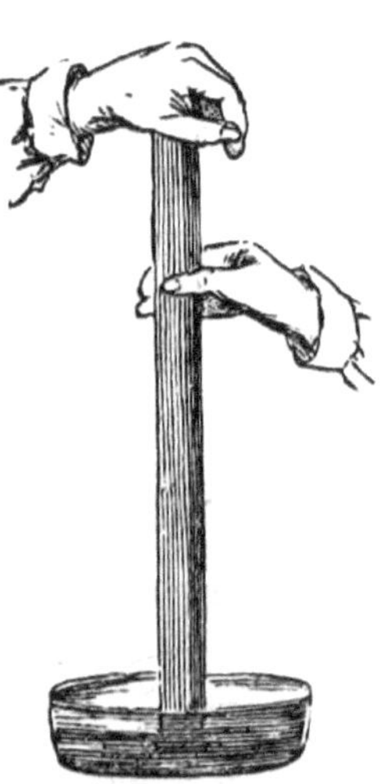

put the other end under water, and hold it as you see here. The water will stay up in the tube as long as you keep the palm of your hand tight over the top of it; but loosen your hand, and the air will go in and push down the water into the vessel.

You can see, from what I have told you, why a vent-hole is needed in a barrel from which we draw any liquid. If the barrel be tapped, the liquid will not run out, unless the air can get in above so as to press it out. Till the vent-hole is made, the liquid will stay in, just as the water stays up in the tube in the experiment. When we make the vent-hole, we do the same to the barrel as we should do to the tube if we should make a little hole in the top of it, or as you do to the tube in the second experiment when you loosen your hand at the top of it to let the air in.

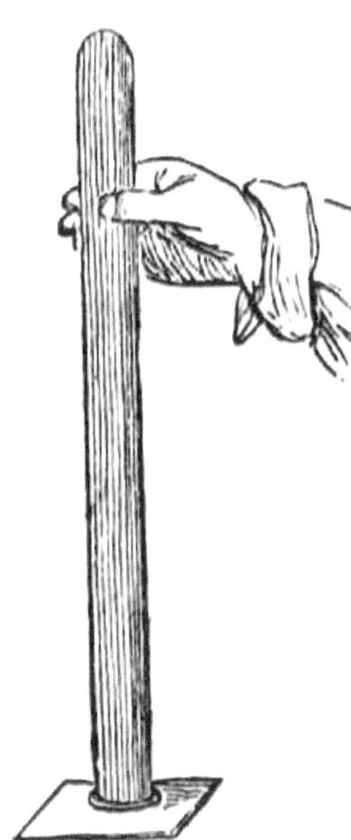

Experiment showing that the air presses upward as much as downward.

This pressure of the air that I have told you about is in every direction. It is upward and sideways as well as downward. This may be shown by another experiment with a glass tube, as represented here. Fill the tube with water, and then place carefully over its open end a smooth slip of paper. You can then turn it over so that the open end shall be downward, as seen in the figure, and the water will not run out. What is the reason of this? It is because the pressure of the air on the paper keeps the water in. We can often succeed with this experiment with a wine-glass, or even a common tumbler, though we can do it more easily with something that has a smaller opening.

But you will ask, perhaps, this question: If it be the pressure of the air that keeps the water from running out, what need is there of the paper? The paper merely serves to keep the surface of the water smooth and whole. If the paper were not there, the air would get in between the parts of the water, and would rush up and force the water out. For the same reason, if, instead of the small hole commonly made in tapping, a large hole be made in the barrel, the liquid will run out without any vent-hole. In this case, the air has a chance to work itself in among the parts or particles[1] of the liquid, and go in bubbles up into the upper part of the barrel. A mere slip of paper put on the hole would keep the liquid in, as in the case of the tube or the wine-glass, and for the same reason. You know that there is a gurgling sound made when a liquid is poured from a jug or a bottle. This is caused by the bubbles of air that pass in while the liquid is coming out.

Questions.—What is said about the air's being every where? Tell about the sponge and the barrel. How is breathing like using a pair of bellows? What is said about the ease with which air is moved out of the way? Give the comparison about going through a crowd. Why is the air pushed out of the way so easily? What is said about wading in water? Tell about the experiment with the glass tube open at one end. Why is a vent-hole needed in a barrel when we want to draw off what is in it? Give the comparison to the experiments with the tube. How can you show that the air passes upward and sideways as well as downward? What does the paper do in this experiment? Why is there no need of a vent-hole when a large opening is made in a barrel? What makes the gurgling when a liquid is poured from a jug or a bottle?

---

1   I explain about the particles of water farther on, in the 16th and 17th chapters.

CHAPTER V.

PUMPS.

YOU KNOW that you can suck up water or any fluid through a straw or any other tube. Now what is it that makes the water go up through the tube into your mouth? I will tell you. When you put the tube into your mouth it is full of air, and so long as the air is there the water will be kept out; but when you suck you remove the air from the tube; and as the air goes out, the water comes in, following right on after the air. But what makes the water come in? Does it come in of itself because there is room made for it? No. Water can not move itself. It must be moved by something else. It is the air pressing on the water in the vessel you are sucking from that pushes it up into the tube. You do not really draw up the water. You get the air out of the way in the tube, and then the air that is all the time pressing on the water in the vessel pushes it up into your mouth. As soon as you stop sucking, and take your mouth from the tube, the water that is in the tube will run down into the vessel, because it is pressed down by the air that goes in at the top of the tube.

You know that you have to suck commonly several times before the water will reach your mouth. If the tube is a very large one, you suck a great many times to get all the air out of it. At first you suck out a little of the air in the tube, and the water is pushed up to take its place; then you suck a little more out, and more water is pushed up, and so on till it reaches the top of the tube. On the following page is a boy that has partly filled his tube, and one more

THE OPERATION OF A PUMP EXPLAINED.

suck would bring the fluid to his mouth.

You can now see how we pump up water out of a well or cistern. The water is not drawn up, but it is pushed up just as it is in the tube when you suck. When you work the handle, you do the same thing for the pump that your mouth does for the tube in sucking any liquid; and when the pump has not been worked for some time, you have to move the handle up and down several times before the water comes, just as you have to suck several times to fill a tube of any length with water.

I will show by some figures how a pump operates. In the first figure the hand is raising the handle, as you know we always do when we begin to pump. The raising of the handle, you see, makes the piston, as it is called, go down in the pump. Here it is going down through air, for the water has not as yet got up as far as the piston. Now, if this piston were a whole solid piece of wood, it would do no good, for it would press the air down before it. But it is not solid. It has a hole through it, and a sort of clapper or valve on the hole. Therefore, as the piston goes down, the air pushes up the valve, and goes up through the hole. You see that this air is shut in between the piston and the water; and when the piston presses down, the only way for

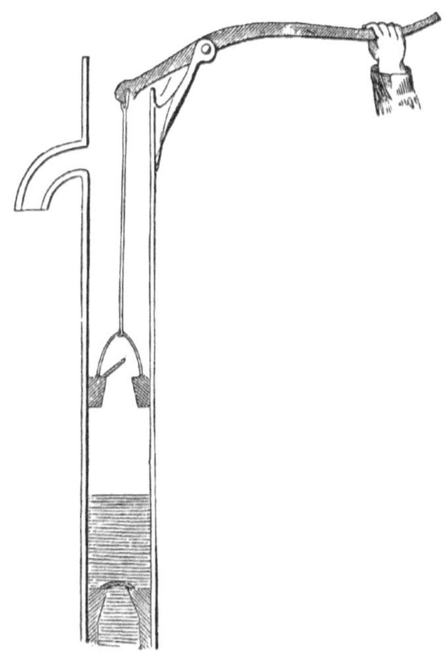

it to get out of the way is to press upon that little door, and go up above the piston.

Well, the handle is up. The next thing is to bring it down, as represented in this picture. As the handle goes down, the piston goes up, as you see. You remember that I told you that, as the piston was going down, as seen in the first figure, some of

the air went up through the hole and got above the piston. Now this air can not get down again, for the moment that the piston begins to move up, the air, pressing on the valve, shuts it down. Now, as the piston goes up, there is room made below it. How is this room filled? The air that is there, as you see, rises up to fill it, and the water follows the air.

The next moving of the piston down will carry

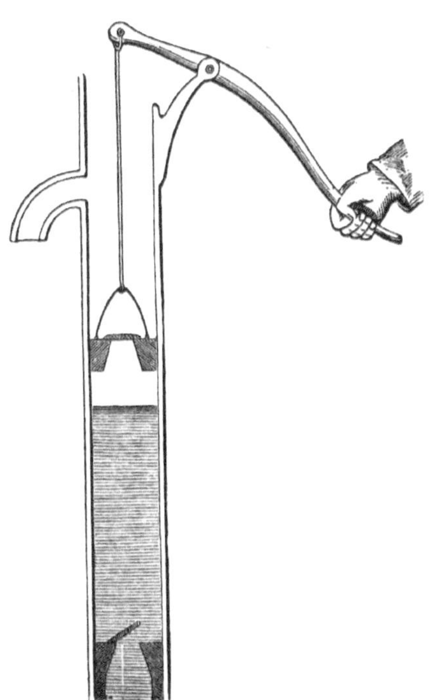

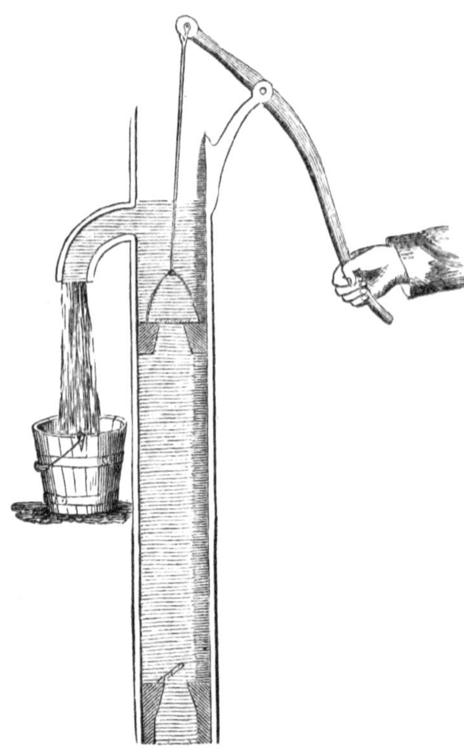

it below all the air and down into the water; and the water will go up through the little door, just as the air has done before it. Then the moving of the piston up will carry this water so high as to make it run out of the mouth of the pump, as seen in this figure.

But there is a valve in the pump that I have said nothing about as yet. This lower valve operates in this way: As the air or the water goes up in the pump, the valve is pushed open by it, as you see in the second figure and in the last one; but when the piston works down, as seen in the first figure, this valve is shut, so that all the water that gets above it is safe, and can not go back.

What is it that makes the air and the water rise in the pump? All that gets above the piston is lifted up by the piston, as you see. But what makes that rise which is below the piston? It is the pressure of the air on the water in the well or cistern. This pushes up the water as fast as there is room made for it.

If a cistern were full of water, and were air-tight also, you could not pump up the water from it. You must have air there to push up the water, or it will not come up when you make room for it by working the pump.

You see, then, that sucking and pumping are very much alike. In the pump the piston makes the room for the air and the water to be pushed up into. Now, when you suck, there is a piston that operates very much as the piston of a pump does. Your tongue is the piston. See how this is. When you suck through a tube held in water, you move your tongue in such a way as to make a space in the mouth, and the air in the tube is pushed in to fill up this space; and when the air is all pushed in, the water is pushed in after it. Both are pushed in, as I have before told you, by the air pressing on the water in the vessel. It is just as water is pushed up into a squirt-gun when you draw the piston. This piston does in the gun, when you draw it, the same thing that your tongue does in your mouth when you move it in sucking. It makes space, and the water is pushed into the gun, as it is into the mouth, to fill up this space. The way in which the space is made in the mouth in sucking is this. Before you begin to suck, the tongue fills the mouth, so as to be up against its roof; but when you suck, you move the tongue down from the roof of the mouth, and this makes a space there; and whatever is in the tube, whether it be air or water, is pushed in to fill this space.

The common language, then, which is used about sucking and pumping is not exactly correct. When we suck or pump, it seems to us as if the liquid was drawn up, and so we use the word draw in regard to it. So, too, we talk about the suction or drawing power. But, as I have showed you, the liquid is pushed up instead of being drawn. All that the piston in a pump does is to make room. It does not draw the water into that room, but the pressure of the air forces it in. Whenever there is any room made, the air is always ready either to go in itself or to force something else in.

Questions.—*Explain* the operation of sucking up water through a tube. Why does the water in the tube run down into the vessel when you stop sucking and take your mouth away? Why is it that you commonly have to suck several times before the water reaches your mouth? How is pumping like sucking? What is shown by the first figure? What by the second? What by the third? Explain the operation of the lower valve of the pump. What makes the air and the water rise in the pump? Why would they not rise if the cistern were full and were air-tight? Explain how the tongue acts as a piston in sucking. Give the comparison about the squirt-gun. What is said about the language used about sucking and pumping?

CHAPTER VI.

THE BAROMETER.

WATER CAN be raised in a pump only to a certain height, and the mistake has sometimes been made of getting the pump so long that it would not work. If it be more than about thirty-four feet from the water up to the piston, the water can not be made to go up so high. What is the reason? It is because the air, pressing on the surface of the water in the cistern or well, will raise it only to the height of thirty-four feet. It does not press hard enough to force it up any higher.

Suppose you had a glass tube over thirty-four feet long, with one end open, and used it as represented in the first experiment in Chapter IV., on page 27. The water would be kept up in it only the thirty-four feet. The weight of a column of water of that height just balances the pressure or weight of the air. Above that height in the tube there would be a space in which there would not be any thing.

Quicksilver or mercury, as perhaps you know, is a fluid like water, but very much heavier. The pressure of the air, therefore, will hold up a column of this not nearly as high as the column of water it holds up. The column of mercury held up in a glass tube is not quite three feet long, while that of water is thirty-four feet.

You can now understand how the instrument called a barometer is made. The object of this is to tell how heavy the air is, for the air is heavier at some times than it is at others. A glass tube, open at one end, and about three feet in length, is taken, and is filled with the mercury. Then the open end is put into a dish of mercury, as seen in the figure. There will be a space in the tube above the mercury, as represented, for the air will support by its pressure a column of only about thirty inches of mercury—six inches less than three feet, the length of the tube. A scale, divided into inches, is added, as seen in the figure; and the whole, neatly inclosed in a case, makes what we call a barometer. This means a measurer of the pressure or weight of the air.

If the barometer be carried up a mountain, the mercury falls. Why is this? It is because there is less height of air pressing on the mercury than there is in the valley below, and of course it will not hold up so long a column of mercury. In the valley, as I have told you in Chapter I., the air is forty-five miles high; and if we carry the barometer up a mountain three or four miles high, it will make a difference of several inches in the height of the mercury in the tube.

I have said that the air is heavier at some times than at others. In a bright, clear day, the air is heavy, and then the mercury rises high, or, rather, is pushed up high in the tube. But when it is cloudy and rainy, the mercury falls, for the air is then lighter than usual, though people often say at such a time how heavy the air is. The truth is that we feel better when the air is clear and heavy, and so the air seems light to us. On the contrary, we do not feel so well when it is cloudy and the air is light.

The barometer is of use to the sailor in telling him of threatened storms; for when a storm is coming the air is light, and the mercury in the barometer falls of course. The sailor, therefore, looks now and then at his barometer, and if he at any time sees the mercury fall suddenly, he gets ready for a storm, for he knows that it may come on very rapidly. Dr. Arnot says that he was once on board of a vessel where the captain was enabled to save his ship and all on board because he took warning in season from his barometer. The sun had just set, and, as the evening was very pleasant, all on board were enjoying themselves in various ways. But the captain's orders were given to take down sails and prepare for a storm. All were astonished, for nobody could see any signs of a storm. But the captain had seen the mercury sink down very suddenly in his barometer, and he knew that trouble was coming, and probably very soon. He hurried the men, therefore, but the storm came before he was quite ready. It was a violent hurricane. But the ship, though much damaged, was saved, and in the morning the wind was still, and all were rejoicing in their deliverance. Probably, if the captain had not looked at his barometer, the ship, with all on board, would have been lost.

Questions.—How high can water be raised in a pump? Why can it not be raised higher? Tell about the experiment with a long glass tube. How high a column of mercury will the pressure of the air hold up? Explain the barometer. Explain the falling of the mercury when the barometer is carried up a mountain. How does the barometer show that the air is heavier at some times than it is at others? Why does the air seem light to us when it is heavy, and heavy when it is light? How is the barometer of use to the sailor? Tell about the storm as related by Dr. Arnot.

CHAPTER VII.

THE AIR-PUMP.

A great many interesting experiments about the pressure of the air can be tried with the air-pump, which you see represented here. This I will describe, so that you may understand how it works. At *a, a*, are two pump-barrels. In them are two pistons with valves, such as there are in common pumps, except that they are made a

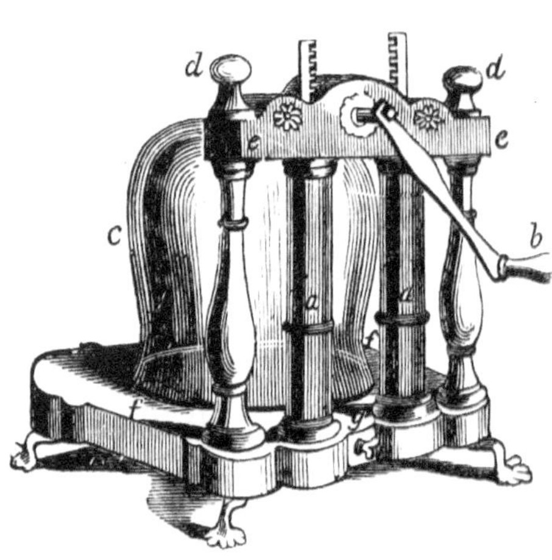

DESCRIPTION OF THE AIR-PUMP.

great deal more nicely. These pistons are worked by the handle, *b*. The frame-work, *e e*, that holds the pump-barrels, is made very strong and firm, so that the pumps may work true. There is a large plate, *f*, of metal, made very even and smooth. At *c* is a large glass vessel, closed at the top, but open at the bottom. Its edge is made very smooth, so that it may fit well on the smooth plate. In the middle of the plate is a hole. This opens into a passage which leads to the bottom of the two pump-barrels.

Now you can see how the instrument works. The two pump-barrels work in the same way that a common water-pump does. With them the air is pumped out of the glass vessel by the passage which leads to them from the centre of the plate. By this means most of the air may be pumped out. If we want to let the air in after pumping it out, we loosen the screw g, for from the opening here there is a passage that leads to the hole in the centre of the plate.

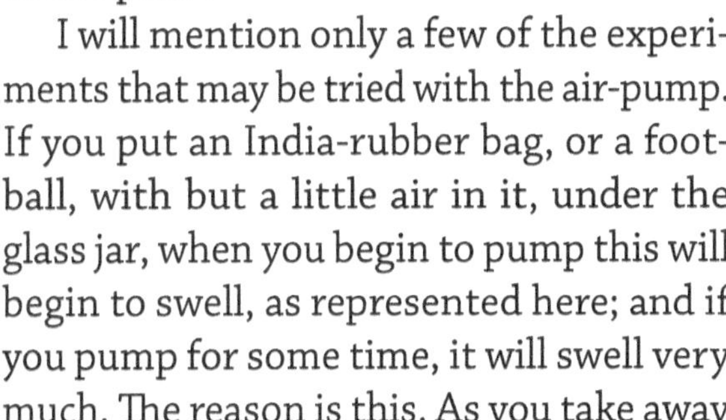

EXPERIMENTS.
INDIA-RUBBER BALL.

I will mention only a few of the experiments that may be tried with the air-pump. If you put an India-rubber bag, or a football, with but a little air in it, under the glass jar, when you begin to pump this will begin to swell, as represented here; and if you pump for some time, it will swell very much. The reason is this. As you take away the air from around the ball, the air in the ball expands. If you then turn the screw that lets the air into the jar, the ball will become small again, because it is pressed upon by the air that is let in.

So, too, if some soap-bubbles be put under the jar, when you pump out the air they will swell; that is, the air shut up in the bubbles will expand, because the pressure of the air around them is lessened.

It is amusing to see a shriveled apple under the jar of the air-pump. After pumping a little it will swell out, and appear like a plump, fresh apple; but let in the air again, and the apple becomes shriveled as before. This is owing to the air that is in the apple, for there is air in every thing. There is air in our bodies; and if the air all about us could be lessened very much, just as it is in the jar of the air-pump, we should swell up like a puff-ball. It is the pressure of the air all around us that keeps us just of the size we are.

The air does more in pressing than you think. As you move about in it, it does not seem to press upon you at all; but it really presses upon you very hard. It presses on you with the weight of about fifteen pounds upon every square inch—that is, a space of this size. It would take many such spaces to cover over your hand. The air really presses upon your hand, as you hold it

out flat, with more than the weight of a hundred pounds. You can hardly believe this, and you will want to know how it is that you do not feel this weight or pressure of the air. I will tell you.

Hold out your hand flat in the air. You know that there is air underneath your hand as well as over it. And this air underneath presses up just as much as that above presses down. Now this is the reason that you do not feel the pressure. If the air underneath your hand could be taken away, you would feel the pressure of that which is above. You would not only feel it, but you could not bear it. This we can prove by the air-pump. Take the jar off from the plate, and then put upon it a small glass vessel, open at both ends, such as you see here. Place your hand over it tightly as represented, and then let some one

How this is borne.

work the pump. Your hand will be pressed down into the cup so hard after a little pumping that you will be glad enough to have the pump stopped and the air let in.

Observe what is done to your hand by the pumping. Some of the air is taken away from beneath your hand— that is all; and, this being done, you feel now the pressure

HOW THE BOY'S SUCKER OPERATES.

of the air above it, because there is no pressure below to balance it.

You can show the same in another way with this glass cup. Tie a piece of bladder or India-rubber over one end of it, and then place this over the hole in the plate of the air-pump. As you pump out the air, the India-rubber will be pressed down into the cup by the air above, as represented here.

The pressure of the air is very well shown by the sucker, as it is called, with which boys sometimes amuse themselves. This sucker is a round piece of leather, with a string fastened to the middle of it. The leather is moistened, and then pressed evenly upon the smooth surface of a stone, and now the stone can be raised, as you see here, by the string, even if it be a pretty large one. But how is it that the leather sticks so fast to the stone? It is by the pressure of the air upon it. When you pull on the string, you raise the middle of the leather a little from the stone, and this makes a little space there in which there is no air. But all the leather around by its edge is pressed very tight upon the stone by the air outside; and it is because no air can get between the leather and the stone that the leather holds on to it so well. If the leather is not pressed down exactly even, or if there be some unevenness in the stone where the leather is put upon it, the air will get in between the leather and the stone, and the sucker will not operate.

Flies and other insects, that walk along so well on the ceiling and on smooth glass, have suckers on their

SUCKERS IN THE FEET OF FLIES.
THE SUCKING-FISH AND THE SHARK.

feet, that work very much in the same way that the boy's sucker does upon the stone. Some fishes have suckers by which they can stick to rocks or any thing else. In this case, it is water that makes the pressure instead of air. Here is the drawing of a fish that has a sucker, or, rather, a set of suckers, on the upper part of its head. With this it can adhere to any thing very firmly. A singular story is told by a traveler about one of these sucking-fishes. He saw a shark attempt to seize it, but the fish dodged him, and then fastened itself to the shark's back by its suckers. It so happened that one of the sailors had tied to the fish a stick of wood by a short line. The shark dashed off with this fish thus fastened to him towing the stick of wood astern. He soon stopped, and, getting hold of the cord, jerked the fish off, and then dove at it as before. The fish dodged him again, and got hold with its suckers a second time, and when last seen, the shark was struggling in vain to get rid of the troublesome fellow.

Questions.—Describe the air-pump, and tell how it works. Tell about the experiment with the India-rubber ball, with the soap-bubbles, and with the shriveled apple. How much is the pressure of the air on every square inch of your body? How much is it on your whole hand? Why do you not feel this pressure? What experiment with the air-pump makes this plain? Give the other experiment that shows the same thing in another way. How is the boy's sucker made? Explain how it holds on to the stone. How do flies and other insects walk on ceilings and on glass? Tell about the sucking-fish.

CHAPTER VIII.
GASES.

I HAVE told you about the air which we breathe, and which is all around us; but there are other kinds of air. When we light the gas, what is it that we set on fire? It is an air, or gas, as we call it, that comes through the pipe to the burner. It is like the air which we breathe in some respects. It is transparent; that is, you can see through it as you can through common air. It moves about as easily as air does. But it is different from the air in some things. It is lighter. The air has no smell; but this gas has a very bad smell, as you may know when it leaks out of the pipes. Air does not burn, but this gas does; and it is curious that when it burns the bad smell is all gone.

Sometimes, when the gas leaks out of a pipe, it is very dangerous. If a closed room should get very full of it, and you should go into it with a light, the gas in the room would all take fire and explode. Persons have been killed in this way. It is well that the gas does smell badly, for this lets us know when it leaks, so that we may guard against the danger. We should let the gas out by opening doors and windows before we bring a light in.

Persons have sometimes been killed by the gas in another way. You know that there is in every gas-pipe something that you can turn so as to shut the pipe, and thus keep the gas from coming out. Now persons that do not know how the gas is managed have blown it out instead of shutting it off. When this is done, the gas continues to come out from the open pipe just as it did when it was burning, and gradually fills the room; and if the person in the room goes to sleep, he will be injured, and perhaps even killed by breathing the gas.

Did you ever think what flame is in a common wood or coal fire? It is burning gas. The heat makes the gas out of the wood or coal, and this takes fire just as the gas does that comes out of the burner when you put a light to it. Sometimes you see a little stream of gas blowing out of some part of a stick of wood, as gas blows out of a burner. It makes quite a noise as it blows. If it is not on fire, you can set fire to it just as you light the gas from a burner.

You see, then, that every fire-place, or grate, or stove is a gas factory; but the gas is burned up as fast as it is made. The gas which is made at the gas-works is made in such a way that it is not burned at the time. It is made generally by heating coal, and is kept in large reservoirs called gasometers. From them pipes branch out in the same way that they do from water-works; and through these the gas goes all about to different buildings, as water goes in aqueduct pipes; and as the water comes out when you open the faucet, so does the gas when you open the burner.

There is one gas that every one ought to know about, because many persons have been killed by it from want of this knowledge. This gas is made whenever charcoal is burned; and many deaths have occurred from it by burning charcoal in small furnaces in closed rooms. This is often done to warm a room where there is no stove or fire-place. As the charcoal burns slowly, the gas is made, and as it is heavier than air, it spreads, at first, all over the floor. It gets higher and higher, and at length reaches the mouths, of the persons in the room. If they happen to be asleep, they are very apt to be killed by breathing the gas; but if they are awake, they are conscious of the unpleasant feelings the gas produces, and either go out into the air, or make some noise which brings others to their relief.

This gas sometimes collects in wells, and kills men that go down into them. Now there is one way by which we can always tell whether this gas is in a well. If there be none there, we can lower a lighted candle down to the water and it will not go out; but if there be any of this gas there, the candle will go out as soon as it reaches it.

There is in Italy a cave or grotto, which is called the Grotto of the Dogs. The reason that this name was given to it will appear from what I will tell you about it. This deadly gas is constantly made there in some way that we do not understand. There is enough of it to reach above a dog's head, but it never gets up as high as a man's head. While a man, then, can breathe in the grotto perfectly well, a dog can not, for he is down in the gas. A dog is kept there by some one living close by, for the purpose of showing the effect on him to visitors. When he is carried into the grotto, he soon falls down, and would die if he were left there; but as they wish to keep him for exhibition to others, they bring him out, and though he looks as if he were dead, dashing some cold water on him and letting him breathe the fresh air soon revive him.

This gas is constantly breathed out from our lungs. It is the bad air that I told you about in Chapter XX., Part First, that leaves take from the lungs of animals, giving them back good air in return. You see, then, how important it is that this gas shall get from us to the leaves, and that the good gas from the leaves shall come freely into our lungs. But this can not be done unless there is a free circulation of the air. When people are shut up in a close room, a great deal of this bad gas is made in a little while, and unless it is let out of the room it does harm. It does not often kill any one at once, but it injures the health; and the poisonous effect repeated every day, though it be but a little, after a while may destroy life. A few persons are killed quickly by this gas made from burning charcoal; but a great many are killed slowly by it as it is given out from their lungs, because they do not take enough pains to let it escape.

Questions.—In what things is the gas that we burn like air? In what does it differ from air? What is said about the smell of gas? In what two ways is life sometimes destroyed by gas? What is flame in a common wood or coal fire? Tell about the blowing we sometimes see in wood on the fire. What is said about the making of gas? What is said about the gas that comes from burning charcoal? How are people sometimes killed by it? What is said about its being in wells? Tell about the Grotto of the Dogs. What is said about the lungs giving out this gas? How does it often do harm when given out in this way? Which kills the most people, the gas that comes from burning charcoal or that which comes from people's lungs?

CHAPTER IX.

POWDER.

POWDER IS a very harmless thing of itself. You can take it into your hand and it will not hurt you; but touch it with fire, and it flashes and explodes; and if there is much of it, it breaks every thing in pieces all around it. When a magazine or a powder-mill blows up, there is great destruction of every thing that is near.

You know that powder is used in blasting rocks. A hole is drilled and the powder is put in. The blaster lights something which will burn very slowly down to the powder, so that he may have time to get out of the way. When the powder explodes, the rock is all broken apart into large and small pieces.

Now, how is it that the powder does all this? It does it by changing all at once into a great quantity of gas. That is all. When you look at some powder, a heap of black grains, there is no gas in it; but the moment that the fire touches it the powder is all gone. But how? Has it become nothing? No; it is changed into something else. The black powder is chiefly gas now. It is not all gas; if it were, you could not see it. The smoke that you see is gas, with something else from the burning powder mixed with it. This gas pushes out every way as soon as it is made, so that it may get room, and it does it so quickly that it carries every thing before it. It does the same that the air does when it moves very quickly, only it moves a great deal more quickly, and so does a great deal more.

This changing of powder into gas is done very quickly—

as quick as a flash, as we say. I knew a boy that once forgot this in using some powder. He put some powder into a log of wood in order to split it; but, instead of fixing a slow match, as men do in blasting rocks, he touched off the powder, intending to get out of the way by running. But the powder was, of course, too quick for him. It blew him over, burning him a little, and frightening him a great deal.

Sometimes water is changed into steam so quickly that it is like the changing of powder into gas in its effects. This is seen in the way that the boiler of a steam-engine is sometimes burst, as I will explain to you. By carelessness, there is not a proper supply of water in it. The fire will, of course, heat the boiler very hot. Now see what must be the consequence when more water is let into it. The boiler, being so very hot, changes this fresh supply of water all at once into steam, and you know it takes but little water to make considerable steam, just as it takes but little powder to make a great deal of gas. All this steam so suddenly made acts precisely like the gas made by burning powder. It must have room, and as there is not room enough for it in the boiler, it must get out somewhere. The strong boiler can not hold so much steam in, and it bursts.

But perhaps you will ask, Is it nothing but air or gas that throws the ball out of the cannon, or the bullet out of the gun, so fast that you can not see it? Can such a light, thin thing as gas drive a ball through even thick beams of wood? Yes, the gas that the powder turns into can do all this.

Now see the reason why the powder and the ball must be put into a cannon to do this. If the powder should be laid upon the ground, with the ball lying upon it, and fire should be touched to it, there would not be much of a sound, and the ball would not be moved much. Why? Because the gas that the powder turns into has a chance to escape in every direction; but when the powder and the ball are put into a cannon, the gas is all shut in, so that it can escape but one way, instead of every way, as it did when the powder was on the ground. It goes out of the mouth of the cannon, pushing the ball before it. It does to the ball just what the air does to you when it blows against you and pushes you along. It is a very hard blowing of gas that throws out the ball so fast. The gas is made all at once, as I have before told you, and it must find room somewhere. There is not room for it in the cannon, and in going out to find room it throws the ball out.

If you should blow a little ball of paper from your mouth, it would not go far. This is for the same reason that a ball laid upon a heap of powder is not moved much when the powder is exploded. But put the paper ball into a quill, and blow through it, and you can send it across a room quite swiftly. The reason is, that the air which you blow out can escape only through the quill, just as it is with the gas in the cannon.

When the gas comes out of the mouth of the cannon, it spreads out in all directions, because it has room now. It is exactly as it is with a crowd of people coming through a door; as fast as the crowd gets through, it spreads out.

Observe, now, how rocks are rent in pieces in blasting. Quite a large hole is drilled into the rock. It is like the space in the barrel of a gun when it is done. This is filled with powder. Why, now, when the powder explodes, does not the gas come out of this in the same way that it does out of a cannon or a gun? Why, instead of this, does it break the rock in pieces? It is because the hole is not large enough for so much gas to come out. If we should put as little powder into it as we do into a gun, the gas would all come out, as it does out of a gun, without breaking the rock at all; but it is filled quite full of the powder, and so a great deal of gas is made. If we should put as much powder into a gun, it would burst like the rock, because there would not be room enough for the escape of so much gas unless it went out slowly, and that it will not do.

Powder is used in various ways. Some kinds of fire-works are made in such a way that the powder does not burn all at once, as it does in a gun or cannon. You know that when a rocket goes up, it is not sent up by one blast of the powder, as a ball is sent out of a gun. The powder is placed in the tail of the rocket, which is so made that the powder burns all the time that it is going up, the last of it making an explosion high up in the air, scattering the sparks which fall in so beautiful a shower. Now, did you ever think just how it is that the rocket is made to go up so swiftly? It is the gas of the burning powder which streams out from its tail all the time that makes it go up. This pushes down against the air, and it is the resistance of the air to this that raises the rocket. It is just as the resistance of the air to the downward stroke of the bird's wings raises the bird. It is also just as, in jumping up off the ground, the resistance of the ground to your feet makes you go up. You press with your feet on the ground, and so the rocket presses with its gas on the air; and so long as gas keeps coming out of its tail to press on the air, the rocket keeps going up. When the gas is exhausted the rocket comes down.

You have sometimes seen whirling wheels in fire-works. The powder in the wheel is arranged as you see here; and as it burns, the resistance of the air to the gas makes the wheel fly around, for the same reason that it makes the rocket go up into the air.

Questions.—*What* is said about powder when no fire touches it? How is the power of burning powder shown? How are its effects produced? What is the smoke from powder? What is said about the quickness with which powder changes into gas? Tell about the boy that split a log of wood with powder. Give the comparison about steam. How is it that the gas made by burning powder makes a ball go out of a cannon or gun so swiftly? Give the comparison of the quill and the ball of paper. Why does the gas from a cannon spread after it gets out? Tell what is said about blasting rocks. Explain how a rocket is made to go up in the air. What is the comparison about flying and about jumping? What is said about the whirling wheel in fire-works?

CHAPTER X.

POP-GUNS.

EVERY BOY and girl has played with a pop-gun, but did you ever think how it works? I will tell you about this.

You know that the cork does not fly out till the rod is pushed a considerable way down into the tube or barrel of the gun, and then it flies out all at once with a popping noise. What makes it fly out? It is not the rod alone, for it does not touch the cork. It is the air that is between the rod and the cork that gives it the push that makes it fly out, and it gives so quick a push as to make the pop.

I will explain this to you a little more particularly. When you put the cork into the end of the gun, the barrel is full of air. Now, if the cork were not in, as you pushed the rod the air would all go out before it; but the cork in the end keeps all the air in. As you push the rod, you crowd the air into a smaller space. If you push the rod half way, then the same air that filled the whole gun has half the room that it had before you pushed the rod. Now, when air is pressed or crowded in this way, it tries, as we may say, to get away from the pressure. In doing this, it presses on the cork; but the cork sticks fast in the mouth of the gun till the pressure is enough to push it out, and when it gives way it does it all at once, and so makes the popping sound. It is as if the air gave the cork a sudden kick, and out it flies.

When I was a boy, we had no such nice pop-guns as boys now have. We had to make them ourselves. We would sometimes make the tube or barrel part out of elder, which, you know, has a large pith. We would sometimes take a quill for a barrel. To this we would fit a stick as a rod. We would then punch each end of the quill through a thin slice of raw potato. This would, of course, leave a round piece of potato in each end. Now, by pushing the rod quickly through the quill, the piece of potato in the farther end would fly out with a pop, in the same way that a cork does from the pop-guns nowadays. You see how this is done. The air which is shut up in the quill between the two pieces of potato is crowded into a small space when the stick is pushed in. It tries to escape from this pressure, and so presses on the potato at the farther end. This gives way all at once and flies out. But why must we have the potato in both ends? It would not be necessary if the stick could be made to fit the quill exactly; but it can not, and so there would be a leaking of air by it if we should have the potato in only one end. The piece of potato in the end where you put in the stick prevents this leaking of air. It makes, in fact, a tight piston for the stick to work.

It is the springiness of the air that makes the pop-gun work. This you can see by some experiments. Fill your pop-gun with water, and see how different from the air it will act. The moment that you push the rod, the cork will be pushed out without any popping, and the water will run out. What is the reason of this? It is because you can not crowd the water, as you do the air, into any smaller room. It moves straight along, and pushes out the cork.

As the water can not be crowded into any smaller space, it has no spring. But the air can be shrunk up, as we may say, by pressure, and it is ready to swell out again whenever it can have a fair chance to do so; and the harder you press it, the greater is this springiness. You can see that this is true by a little experiment that you can try with your pop-gun.

Press the cork end of the gun firmly against something, so that the cork can not come out. Now push in the rod quickly, and then let go of it. It will fly back, because the crowded air, by a spring, throws it back. And the harder you push it in, the more forcibly will it fly back.

Now, if you try the same experiment with the water in the gun, you will find that you can not push the rod unless the gun leaks, and then the water will come back by the piston. Why is this? It is because the water can not be crowded into any smaller space, as the air can be. If it could be, the water would do just as well in the pop-gun as air does.

You see, then, that it is the spring of the air that forces the cork out of the gun; and the air has this spring because it is pent up and crowded together, as we may say, into so small a space. It wants more room, and pushes to get it.

The cork is shot out of the pop-gun in the same way that the ball is shot out from the cannon. The air, pent up in a little space in the pop-gun, does the same thing as the gas, pent up in the cannon, does. The air wants more room, and so it kicks out the cork; and the gas, so suddenly made out of the powder, wants more room, and so it kicks out the ball. The gas has the same springiness that the air has.

It is this springiness of the air, called its elasticity, that makes the foot-ball bound so. If the ball were filled with water instead of air, it would not bound at all, because the water has no elasticity.

I have told you that the more the air is pressed the greater is its springiness. In what is called the air-gun, a great deal of air is crowded into a very small space—much more than there is in a pop-gun; and a bullet can therefore be fired from it with force enough to go through a board. It is done in this way: The pressed air is shut up tight, and all at once it is let into the barrel of the gun where the bullet is. It throws the bullet out just in the same way that the gas of the powder does in a common gun. This air-gun is only a curiosity. It will never come into use, for it is quite a tedious operation to load it with pressed air. The common gun, you know, is very easily loaded with powder, and the gas which it turns into does the work even better than the pressed air in the air-gun.

Questions.—What makes the cork fly out of the pop-gun? Explain just how the pop-gun operates. Tell how the quill pop-gun is made. Why do we have the potato in both ends of the quill? What is said about the springiness of the air? How would the pop-gun work if it were filled with water? Why is this? Give the experiment with the pop-gun showing how springy the air is. How is it when you try the same experiment with the gun filled with water? Give the comparison between your pop-gun and a cannon. What is said about the foot-ball? Tell about the air-gun. Why is this not in common use?

CHAPTER XI.

BALLOONS AND BUBBLES.

WHAT IS it that makes a balloon go up in the air? It is because it is so light, you will say; but what it is made of is not as light as air is. It will not, you know, fly off into the air before it is filled. It is what it is filled with, then, that makes it so light.

The balloon is filled with a gas that is much lighter than the air is around it. This makes it so light that it flies up in the air very rapidly, and to a great height; and if the balloon is very large, it can carry up a person, or even two or three persons, in a sort of car or boat attached to it, as represented on the following page.

The car is attached to the balloon in this way: A netting covers the balloon, and the cords that hold the car are fastened to this netting. It would not do, you know, to fasten them to the balloon itself, for that is made of such light material that the cords would tear out with the slightest pull upon them.

How do you think the person in this car manages when he wants to come down? So long as all the light gas remains in the balloon, it will stay up in the air. So, when he wants to come down, he lets out some of this gas. He does this very carefully; for, if he lets out too much, he will go down too fast. Sometimes he will go down too fast in spite of all his care. He is prepared for this, however, in two ways. There are sand-bags in the car, which he can throw out when the balloon is falling too fast. This makes the car so much lighter that it commonly relieves the difficulty; but

HOW THE BALLOON IS PREVENTED FROM GOING DOWN TOO FAST.
THE PARACHUTE.

if it does not, he can use the parachute. This is a sort of umbrella, made very large and very strong. It is represented on the following page both as shut and as opened. You can see how the resistance of the air against this when open would make him go down much slower than he would go without his parachute.

Balloons are sometimes used in warfare, to observe battle-fields, or send messages to and from besieged cities. They were so used in our own war and at the recent siege of Paris. They will probably never come into use in

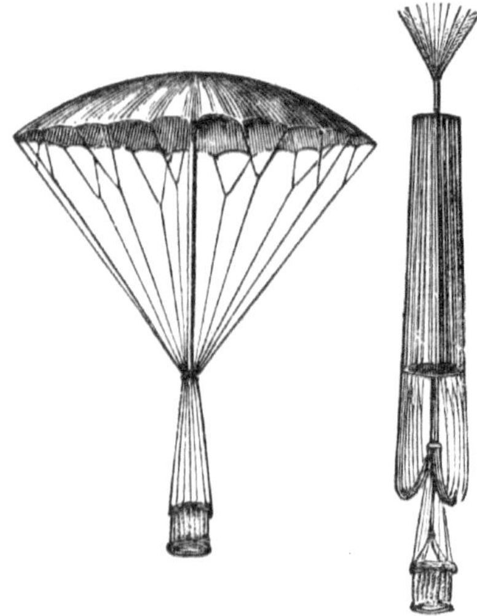

traveling; for, besides the expense and danger, a balloon will always go with the wind, and you never can tell just how the wind blows very high up in the air. It may blow there in a direction wholly different from what it does below, close to the earth. An Englishman, Major Money, went up in a balloon, with the wind blowing from the sea; and he supposed that he should be carried far into the country, and come down safely upon dry land. All was right till he had got up about a mile. Then suddenly the balloon changed its course, and went out toward the sea. This was because the wind up there blew in a direction just opposite to that of the wind below. This wind took him far out to sea, and when he came down he was nine miles from the land. He came near being drowned. He held on to the cords of his balloon, as you see here, for some time. After a while, a vessel came to his relief, and took him on board. As such dangers attend going up in balloons, it is wrong for any one to do it.

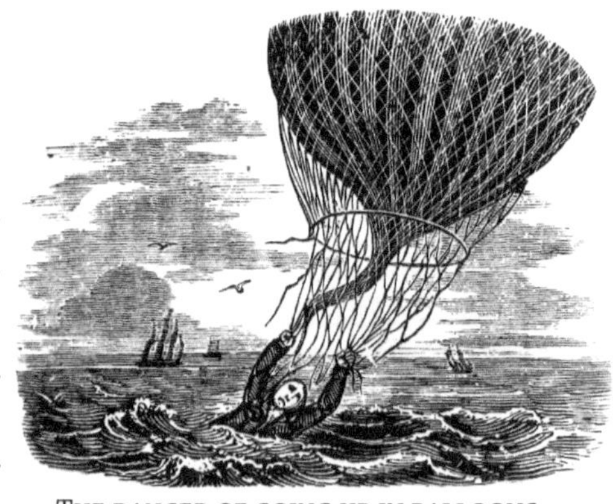

THE DANGER OF GOING UP IN BALLOONS.
A GREAT ESCAPE.

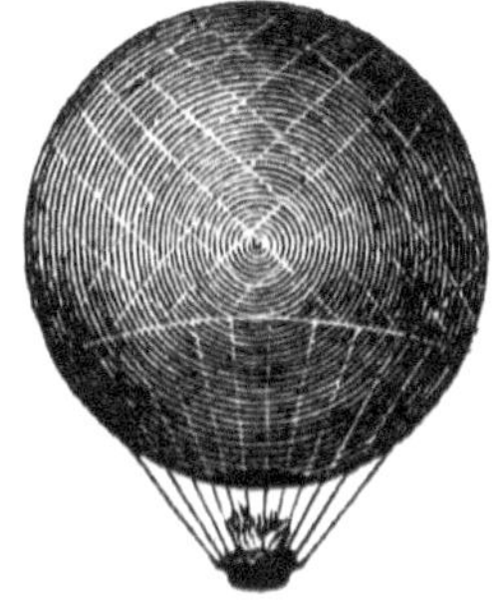

THE HOT-AIR BALLOON.

You can fill a balloon with common air so as to make it fly up like the gas balloon; but the air must be heated to do this. A boy can make such a balloon very easily out of thin paper. He pastes the paper together so as to shape it like a balloon, leaving one end open. It can be filled with hot air by holding it over something burning, with its open end down. It is sometimes done in another way. A sponge wet in turpentine or alcohol is fixed under the opening of the balloon by a little frame-work, as represented above; and if the balloon goes up with the sponge still burning, it will stay up longer than it will if the sponge goes out before it is let off, because the air will keep heated longer.

It is because heated air is so much lighter than the air around it that a balloon filled in this way goes up; but such a balloon comes down soon. It will not keep up so long as a gas balloon will. Why is this? It is because the heated air in the balloon becomes cooled, and then it is no longer lighter than the air around it. The balloon itself is heavier than air, and it goes up and stays up only when it is full of something which is lighter than air.

Children often make balloons in another way. They make them of soap and water, as you see here;

HOW SOAP-BUBBLES ARE LIKE BALLOONS.

for the soap-bubble that flies up in the air is really a balloon; and how beautiful a one it is! How thin and delicate is the covering of this ball of air! It is a sheet of nothing but soap and water, and a touch breaks it; but it answers the purpose. It holds the air, and away it flies.

Now what is the reason that the bubble flies up a little way and then comes down? It flies up because the air in it is slightly heated, and so is lighter than the air around it. It is heated or warmed air, because it comes from the warm lungs of the person that blows the bubble. But it soon becomes cool, and then the bubble comes down, just as the balloon filled with hot air does when the air in it becomes cool.

There are some things to be noticed about this ballooning with soap and water. The water must be warm, or your little balloons will not go up. Why is this? If the water is cold, it will cool the air that comes from your warm lungs, and so your soap and water balloon will be filled with cold air instead of warm air. It will therefore drop to the floor when you expect to see it go up. So, too, the bubbles will not go up so easily and so high in a warm room as they will in cold air. The greater the difference is in warmth between the air in the bubble and that around it, the better it will go up.

The reason of this is plain. The cooler the air is, the heavier it is; and the warmer the air inside of the bubble, the lighter is the bubble; and the very light bubble goes up quickly in the heavy cold air for the same reason that any light thing, like cork, rises very quickly in water. Why it is that light things go up in the air and the water I shall explain in the next chapter.

Questions.—*What* is it in a balloon that makes it so light? How is the car attached to the balloon? How does the person in the car manage when he wants to come down? What does he do if he is coming down too fast? What is a parachute, and of what use is it? Why will balloons never be used for traveling? Tell about the Englishman. Tell about the air balloon. Why will not this stay up as long as the gas balloon? How do children often make balloons? Why does the soap-bubble go up a little way and then come down? Why is it that the bubbles do not go up if you use cold water? Why will they go up better in the cold air than they will in a warm room?

CHAPTER XII.

MORE ABOUT BALLOONS.

HERE IS a balloon which was contrived in 1670, two hundred years ago, by a man whose name was Lana. You would suppose, from the picture of it, that it would go very well with its large sail for the wind to blow it along. There are, you see, four large balls. These, made of copper, were hollow. The air was to be pumped out of them, so that they might be very light. Now with this balloon Lana did not expect to go up very high, but to travel along considerably above all the houses and hills, just in the direction in which the

wind would carry him by his sail. But his plan, though it looks well, as you see, on paper, failed. The reason was this. If the balls were made quite thin, the air outside would burst them in as soon as the air in them was pumped out; and if they were made thick enough to prevent this, they were so heavy that the balloon would not go up. From what I have told you in the chapter on the air-pump, you will understand why the balls, when made thin, were burst in by the outside air.

The first successful attempt at ballooning was made by Montgolfier, a Frenchman, in 1783. His invention was that of the hot-air balloon, or fire balloon, as it is often called. An improvement on this is to fill the balloon with a light gas instead of hot air. It is in this kind of balloon that persons go up, though some have gone up in the hot-air balloon.

I have not yet told you the real cause of the rising of the balloon in the air. Why, you will say, it is because it is so light, and light things always rise. But what makes light things rise? That is the question.

Light things do not go up of themselves. The birds and the insects, as I have told you in Part II., make themselves go up by working their wings with their muscles. But light things that have no life can not rise of themselves. They are pushed up. And when any light thing has got up as high as it can go, it stops merely because it can not be pushed any higher.

But how are balloons and other light things pushed up? This I will now explain to you. The air around the balloon is heavier than the balloon itself, which is filled with a light gas, or with air that is light because it is heated; and so the air is trying all the time, as we may say, to get below the balloon. In doing this, it pushes up the balloon; and the balloon continues to be pressed upward till it comes to air that is as light as the balloon is. If it be a gas balloon, it will remain there till some of the gas is let out; and if it be a hot-air balloon, it will stay there till the heated air begins to cool.

Now, when the balloon goes down, it is because it has become heavier than the air around it. It goes down because it tries, as we may say, to get underneath the lighter air. In going up, the air pushed it up; but now the balloon pushes the air up. The balloon presses the air that is below it out of the way so as to get under it. This is what it keeps doing all the way as it comes down.

I can make this clear by a comparison. Take a long phial. Before you put any thing into it, you know it is filled with air. Pour some oil into it. The oil is in the bottom of the phial, and the air is above the oil. The reason is that the oil, being heavier than the air, has gone down through it, and has pushed the air up from the bottom of the phial and taken its place there. It has done to the air in the phial what the falling balloon does to the air below it. Now pour a little water in. This will do to the oil as the oil did to the air. It will go down to the bottom, pushing the oil up above it; for water, you know, is heavier than oil. If you pour now some quicksilver into the phial, this heavy fluid will go down and push the water up above it.

You see, in this experiment, that what is heaviest always goes to the lowest place, and so pushes up out of the way what is lighter. The oil pushed up the air; then the water pushed up the oil; and then, again, the quicksilver pushed up the water. And now you have all the four things in the phial in their order. The heaviest, the quicksilver, is at the bottom, and next is the water, and next the oil, and the lightest, the air, is at the top.

If you cork the phial and shake it well, you mix quicksilver, water, oil, and air all together. Then, if you let it stand, you see a good deal of confusion among them as they push to get their places. In getting right again, each pushes up above it what is lighter than itself. The struggle, as we may say, is to get the lowest place. Every thing, no matter how light it is, stays down as low as it can till it is pushed up.

Now what you see with these different things in a phial is true of different kinds of air, or gases. A heavy gas takes the lowest place, while a lighter one goes up, or, rather, is pushed up. You remember that I told you, in Chapter VIII., about a gas that is sometimes in the bottom of wells, just above the water. This gas is heavier than air, and so it stays at the bottom of the well, below the air, as the oil in the phial lay between the lighter air above and the heavier water below. If it were lighter than air, as the gas is with which balloons are filled, the air would go down to the bottom of the well and push up this gas, for the same reason that the oil in the phial pushed up the air, and the water pushed up the oil, and the quicksilver pushed up the water.

This gas can be poured out of a vessel very much as you would pour water out of it. A pretty experiment with it is to pour it out upon a lighted candle. It will flow down upon the flame and put it out. In doing this, it pushes up the air that is around the candle.

Now you can see how the balloon is pushed up into the air. If a gas is set loose that is lighter than air, it will be pushed up in the air in the same way that, in the phial, air is pushed up by the oil, or the oil by the water; and so the balloon, filled with the light gas, is pushed up by the air. It makes no difference whether the gas is loose or is in a light silk bag; in either case it will be pushed up. If loose, it will be scattered about as it is pushed up; if in the bag or balloon, it will be kept together.

A cork rises in water for the same reason that a balloon rises in air. The balloon is pushed up by the air around it because it is lighter than the air, and so the cork is pushed up by the water because it is lighter than the water. As you hold the cork under water, your hand does to it what the fastenings do to the balloon: it keeps it from being pushed up. And when the fastenings of the balloon are let go, away it flies in the air, as the cork flies up in the water when you let go of it.

When the cork gets to the surface of the water, it stops. It will not go up in the air simply because it is heavier than air. But if you put a bag full of light gas in the water and let it go, it will not stop, like the cork, when it gets to the surface, but will keep on going up because it is lighter than air, and so the air pushes it up just as the water did.

Questions.—*Do* light things, like balloons, rise in the air of themselves? Tell about Lana's balloon. Why did it not succeed? Who invented the hot-air balloon? How many years ago was it? What kind of balloon is used for going up into the air? What makes it rise? How is it that the air pushes up a balloon? What makes the balloon go down? What does it do to the air in going down? Tell about the experiment with a long phial? How is it if you shake the phial well? What is said about gases? Tell about the gas which is sometimes in wells. Tell about the experiment with a candle. What becomes of a gas that is lighter than air when it is set free? Does it make any difference whether it is loose or is in a silk bag? Give the comparison of the balloon and the cork.

CHAPTER XIII.

HEATED AIR.

BALLOONS ARE sometimes, as I have told you, filled with heated air. This heated air is lighter than the cool air around it, and so the balloon rises, or, rather, is pushed up. Now observe why the heated air is lighter than the cool air. It is because the heat swells the air, or *expands* it, as it is commonly expressed. The heat, in expanding it, makes it thinner, and of course it is lighter.

You can see by a little experiment that heat swells or expands air. Lay a bladder, partly filled with air, before the fire. The heat will fill out the bladder, making it plump and hard, for it will expand the air that is in it; and if the bladder is already filled with air before you lay it down on the hearth, the swelling air will burst the bladder.

You remember that I told you about putting an apple under the jar of an air-pump. If the apple is shriveled, the moment that you begin to pump the air from around it the apple begins to swell out, because the air in it swells or expands. In this experiment the air in the apple expands because the pressure of the air around it is lessened by its becoming thinner. Now the air in the apple can be made to expand in another way—by applying heat. If you observe an apple put down to the fire for roasting, you see that it swells. If it happens to be rather wilted, the swelling of it will be very manifest; it will become as plump as it would in the air-pump when the air is pumped out. This is because the air in it is expanded by the heat. And when it sputters, it is the expanded air that throws out some of the juice through the broken skin.

You know that, if you roast chestnuts, they pop open with quite a noise, and sometimes fly half across the room. This is owing to the expansion of the air in the chestnut by the heat. This air is shut up in the tight skin of the chestnut; and when it is considerably swelled by the heat, it makes the skin give way all at once, and so produces the popping noise. This is because of the springiness or elasticity of the air. That I have explained before. If you prick a hole in the skin of the chestnut before you put it down to the fire, there will be no popping, for the air will gradually escape from this hole as fast as it is expanded. This hole is to the chestnut what the safety-valve is to a steam-engine. The engine will not burst while the steam can go out by the valve, and so the chestnut, with a hole for the air to get out, does not burst. In the case of both the apple and the chestnut, there is steam mixed with the air. The steam comes from the moisture in the apple and the chestnut, and this has the same springiness that air has, and so helps to produce the effect. I shall tell you about steam in another chapter.

Heated air always rises, for the same reason that a light gas rises. It is pushed up by the cold air, which is heavier. In warming a room, the cold air is constantly pushing the warmed air up, and the air is always warmer in the upper part of the room than it is near the floor. So, also, it is warmer in the galleries of a church than it is in the body of the house, as you perhaps have sometimes noticed.

Around a stove-pipe, the motion of the heated air as it goes up is very manifest. Light things are often seen flying up in the current of the air about the pipe. Sometimes, for amusement, little paper wind-mills are fastened to a stove-pipe, the heated air whirling them around as it strikes them in going up. I have seen a very curious toy, in which a wood-sawyer is made to work by the whirling of a little paper wind-mill. Whenever there is a strong current of hot air, the wind-mill turns quite rapidly, and this sets the sawyer to working his paper saw most furiously. The little figure goes through the motions of sawing very perfectly. It has sawed into the middle of the log, but never gets any farther.

The stream or current of air about a stove-pipe is made by the cooler air, which pushes up that which is warm. As fast as the air is heated by the pipe, cooler air takes its place by pushing it up out of the way; and then this air, coming thus near the pipe, gets heated, and is pushed up in its turn by some more air. As this is constantly going on, there is a constant upward current of air; and the hotter the pipe is, the more rapid is the current, because it heats the air so quickly and so much.

You know, in a house heated by a furnace, how the heated air comes up from the registers. This air is pushed up. As soon as the air around the furnace is heated, cool air comes in to push it up out of the way, and then this cool air is heated and is pushed up by more cool air, and so on. The heated air escapes from the pressure of the cool air by going up in the large tin pipes. The cool air is always driving the warm up, just as it is with the air about a stove-pipe.

Whenever a great fire occurs, after it has continued some time, the wind rises, as it is expressed; though perhaps it blew very gently at first, now it blows very hard. What is the reason of this? It is because the air just about the fire becomes much heated, and therefore very light. The cold air all around rushes therefore toward the fire, just as it does toward a stove or a fire-place in a room, and pushes the light heated air up. In doing this it becomes itself heated, and is pushed up by other cold air, and so on. In this way the air all around the fire is set in motion toward it, and the hotter the fire the more brisk is this motion—that is, the harder does the wind blow. I shall tell you something about the way in which heat makes winds in another chapter.

Questions.—Why is heated air lighter than cool air? What experiment shows that heat expands air? Tell about the shriveled apple. Why do chestnuts often pop open when they are roasted? How can you prevent their popping? Give the comparison of the safety-valve. In warming a room, what is done to the heated air? What is said about the galleries of a church? What is said about the air around a stove-pipe? Tell about the paper wind-mills and the wood-sawyer. How is the current of air about a stove-pipe made? What makes the hot air come up from the registers of a furnace? Why does the wind rise in a great fire?

CHAPTER XIV.
CHIMNEYS.

YOU HEAR people sometimes say of a chimney that it *draws* well, as if the smoke were in some way drawn up the chimney. This is not so. It is pushed up. Smoke is mostly heated air and gas. What you see in the smoke is something from the wood that is carried up in the heated air, in the same way that down or any light thing is carried up by the heated air around a stove-pipe. It is this part of the smoke which you can see that makes the soot. The heated air is pushed up the chimney by the cooler air in the room. It is done in this way: The air close to the fire is heated; the air next to it presses it up, and then gets heated itself, and is pressed up by some more air that comes in its turn to be heated, and so on. In this way there is a constant stream of air up the chimney, just as there is around a stove-pipe.

The air in a room where there is a fire is ever pushing toward the fire; and air is coming into the room, too, in every way that it can get in, to take the place of that which goes up the chimney. It comes through the door when it is opened, and through every crack and crevice. If you hold a light near the fire-place, the flame will bend toward it, because the air is pressing that way. If you hold it near a crack, the air that is coming in will blow it toward you.

If there are two rooms connected by folding-doors, with a fire-place in each, when a fire is made in one alone, cold air will come down the other chimney; for, as the air in the room, as I have told you, is all moving toward the fire, the cold air comes in wherever it can get in to take its place. A lady of my acquaintance was once in great trouble because she did not understand this. Her house was filled with smoke. It happened in this way. There were two rooms connected by folding-doors. A fire had been built in one fire-place, and, after this was well agoing, a fire was built in the other; but the moment this second fire was lighted, the smoke puffed out into the room. How was this? It was pushed out by the cold air coming down the chimney. The lady sent for a neighbor who understood about such things, and he relieved her of the trouble at once. He shut the folding-doors, and opened a window in the room where the fire-place smoked, and now the smoke went directly up the chimney. After the fire had been burning for a little time, and had warmed the chimney, the folding-doors were opened, and both fires burned well.

The reason of all this, I suppose, is plain to you. While the folding-doors were open, there was a movement of the air in both rooms toward the fire first kindled, and so the cold air came down the chimney where there was no fire. When the fire, therefore, was kindled in the second fire-place, this cold air, coming down, blew the smoke out, and would not let it go up to warm the chimney. But when the doors were closed between the rooms, there was a stop put to all this. The movement of the air toward the fire first made was now confined to that one room. There could no air come from the other room now. And then opening the window let in cold air that pushed the smoke up the chimney of this room at once.

You can now understand why it is that we open a door or window to stop the smoking of a fire-place. It is because we want the help of some more cold air to push the smoke up. In some fire-places we can never make a fire without its smoking, unless we have a door or a window open a little while at first. The reason that the fire is not apt to smoke after it has been going some time is that the chimney has become well heated, and so makes the air very thin and light as it goes up; and the lighter the air is, you know, the more easily it is pushed up, just as you can raise a bag of feathers more easily than you can raise a block of wood.

One thing more I must tell you about the cold air coming into a room where there is a fire. Suppose that you open a door into a cold entry. Now, if you hold a light near the floor by the open door, the flame will be blown inward; but if you hold it up at the top of the door, it will be blown outward toward the entry. Why is this? It is because the cold air of the entry comes in at the lower part of the opening, while some of the warm air of the room goes out at the upper part to take the place of the cold air that comes in. The warm air is above the cold air, because it is lighter. It is the cold air coming in that blows the light when you hold it low down, and it is the warm air going out that blows it when you hold it up high. The warm air that goes out is less in quantity than the cold air that comes in. The reason is that there is cold air coming into the entry all the time from outdoors, by every crevice and hole, and this, in part, supplies the place of the air that goes in from the entry to the room. The flame, therefore, is not blown as strongly when you hold the light above as when you hold it below.

I told you in Chapter I. that nothing will burn without air. The air that presses toward a fire feeds it, as it is expressed. It does not all go up the chimney as heated air. Some of it is used in the burning of the wood and coal; and what goes up the chimney is, as I have told you in the first part of this chapter, partly heated air and partly gas.

Now a fire will not burn well unless it has a free supply of air. Fresh air must keep coming to it to feed it. But this can not be unless there is a good upward current from the fire. Firemen very well understand this in putting out fires. If the fire be inside of a building, the more shut up it can be kept the less rapidly will the fire spread, and the more easily can it be put out. If all the doors should be opened, and the windows broken out, the fire would rage, because the air would come in freely at the doors and lower windows, and go out freely at the upper windows. The fire would then have the same upward current that it has in a chimney. I will relate to you an anecdote, which will show how much can be saved by understanding such things. A fire was discovered early one morning by a flickering light shining through the windows in the upper room of a shop. An acquaintance of mine was among the first to get there, and he found a man about to beat the door in with an axe, so as to get at the fire. He kept him from doing this, and would not let him touch the door till they had got a good supply of water on hand. After he was satisfied that there was enough water to put out the fire, he then let the man use the axe, and they rushed up and easily put out the fire. If he had let him break open the door at first, it would have let in the air to feed the fire, and the fire would have got well agoing before the water was brought; and, as it was in a block of wooden buildings, we should have, had a great fire.

The brisker the upward current of a fire is, the more briskly does the fire burn. This is the reason that foundries and other factories, where they want a very hot fire, have such tall chimneys. The air and gas in such a chimney are kept hot for some time, instead of being cooled by spreading out in the open air. The current, therefore, up the chimney is very rapid, and so fresh air comes rapidly to the fire, and makes it burn very briskly. For the same reason, a very brilliant light is given by those lamps that have tall glass chimneys. The wick is thus made to burn briskly.

Questions.—*Why* does smoke go up a chimney? What is smoke? What is there in smoke that you can see? What is soot? Tell how it is that the smoke is pushed up the chimney. What is said about the air in a room where there is a fire? What will happen to a light if you hold it near the fire-place? What if you hold it near a crack in the wall of the room? Tell about the rooms with folding-doors between them. Why do we open a door or a window to stop the smoking of a fire-place? Why is a fire-place not apt to smoke when the fire has been going for some time? Tell about holding a light at the lower part and at the upper part of a door that opens out into a cold entry. How is some of the air that presses toward a fire used? What is necessary to have a fire burn well? What is said about a building that is on fire inside? Tell the anecdote about the fire in a shop. Why do some factories have tall chimneys? What is said about the chimneys of some lamps?

CHAPTER XV.

USES OF WATER.

WHAT A beautiful thing is water! How pure and clear, like a crystal! How "sparkling and bright it is," as you see its ripples in the sun! How we admire it, as it is gathered in little dew-drops on the flowers and leaves in the morning! What a beautiful mirror the water makes when the wind is hushed, showing us on its smooth surface the trees, the houses, and every thing upon the shore!

And what beauty water has when the cold turns it into crystals in the ice, the snow, and the frost! It is the same pure, clean thing then as it is when it runs in the brook, or forms the dew-drop, or falls in the gentle shower.

How useful, too, water is! It is the world's cleanser. It washes every thing. See how dusty every thing looks after a long dry time. Even the grass and the leaves are covered with dust. But let a brisk shower come, and how changed the scene! The trees, the flowers, and the grass look as clean, and fresh, and bright as the washed face of a beautiful child.

And then how the animals love to wash themselves in the water! See the dog rush into it, and then, on coming out, give himself a thorough shaking. It would be well if all children would be as fond of being clean as he is. It is amusing to see the canary bird take his morning bath in his cup of water. How he makes the water fly as he flutters his wings!

Did you ever think that the air every once in a while needs a washing? It does, just as much as you do and every thing else in the world. Even when it seems clean as you look up through it, there are some things in it that would be very bad for us if they remained there. They would produce disease in us. They would be injurious also to other animals, and even to plants. The air, therefore, must every now and then have a washing to purify it; and every time that it rains you can think of the air as taking a shower-bath for this purpose. You see, then, how true it is that water is the world's cleanser. It washes every thing, even the air.

But, besides being the world's cleanser, water is the world's drink. It is the drink of plants as well as of man and animals. The plants drink it from the ground by the mouths in their roots. A great part of the sap, as I have told you in Part I., is water.

We use water so constantly as a drink that we do not think how good and refreshing it is. We think of this once in a while when we happen to be very thirsty. When one is parched with fever, he thinks of cold water as the very best thing on the earth; and when he is asleep, he dreams of the well or spring from which he drank so often in his childhood. A lady who was sick with yellow fever, far away from home, in her delirium talked continually about a pump that was behind a house she had long lived in, some time before this, and kept calling for water from that pump.

The salt water of the sea, you know, is not fit for drinking. And you have heard of persons in a shipwreck escaping in a boat from a sinking ship, and then living almost without food and water for many days. How careful are they not to waste any of the water which they happen to have! Each drinks but little, though they are suffering greatly with thirst. And when it is all gone, they would give any thing for the smallest draught of fresh water. So dreadful is the suffering from thirst that water is almost the only thing which they think of. They wish that it would rain, so that they might catch some water. There is water all around them, but it seems to mock them with its briny waves. It is not the water which they want; they know that it would do no good to drink it.

One who had been in a boat for some days without water said that it seemed to him always after as if it was wrong to waste pure fresh water, and he never could use it as freely as he did before his shipwreck. How thankful should we be that God has given it to us so abundantly that we can commonly use it without stint or measure. It is one of his most precious gifts, and yet it is so common that, when we want to speak of any thing as being very free and abundant, we say that it is as free as water.

But we do not merely drink water. It is mixed up with every thing that we eat. There is much water in all fruits. There is so much in the watermelon that it gives it its name. It is almost all water, with a little sugar in it. Much of the sap in plants and trees is water; so, also, it is with the blood. It could not run in the arteries and veins if there was not water in it. More than three quarters of your blood is water. There is much water, too, in the air. So you see that water is every where, just as the air is.

But I have not told you all the uses of water. The running water turns the water-wheels by which the machinery in mills and factories is put in motion. We sail about on the water in boats, and ships, and steamers. The steam-engines are worked by water changed into steam.

We must not forget the multitudes of fishes and other animals that live in the water, as we do in the air. There is a world of life in the water. It is so much out of sight that we do not think much about it. We only get glimpses of this water-world now and then, and do not think how many animals there are that live in the brooks, and rivers, and ponds, and seas. Besides the fishes that swim in the water, there are multitudes of animals that live on the bottom. There are oysters, and clams, and lobsters, that you are familiar with; and there are multitudes of animals that live in their beautiful shell houses, some of which are very small, and almost as countless often as the sands with which they are mingled.

Questions.—*What* is said about the beauty of water? What is said about its being the world's cleanser? Tell about the dog and the canary bird. What is said about the air's being washed? How do the plants drink water? Do we commonly think how good a drink water is? Tell about the lady sick with fever. What is said about the salt water of the sea? What about the suffering from thirst so common with shipwrecked persons? Tell about the feeling of one who had suffered in this way. What is said about the abundance of water? What is said about water's being in every thing? How much of your blood is water? Mention some more uses of water. What is said about the animals that live in water?

CHAPTER XVI.

WATER ALWAYS TRYING TO BE LEVEL.

IF YOU look at water in a bowl, you see that its surface is smooth and level. If now you stir it about, you make it uneven. Watch it as it becomes still and smooth again. There seems to be a kind of struggle as all the particles of water take their places.

But you will ask me what I mean by the particles of water. We suppose that water is made up of exceedingly fine balls. These balls or particles are so round and smooth that they move among each other very easily. This is the reason that water runs so readily, and so soon becomes level when nothing is disturbing it. If the particles were not so smooth, they would rub each other. They would not roll over each other so freely as they do.

To make this plain, we will compare water to small shot. If you put these into a bowl, they will not lie level, as water does. Now what is the reason that these round balls of lead do not act as the smaller round balls of the water do? It is because they are not as smooth. They can not roll over each other easily, for they rub together. They can not in any way be made as smooth as the particles of water are.

If you pour the shot from one bowl into another, they will run somewhat as the water does; but they will not slip along as easily, for they rub each other as they go, while there is almost no rubbing among the particles of water.

The balls or particles of water are exceedingly small. They are so small that no one has ever seen them. How, then, you will ask, do we know that they are round and smooth? We say that they are, because we can not see how they could move about among each other so easily if they were rough, or had corners or points on them. You can not roll about blocks or nails as you can roll shot; and the smoother the shot the more easily they will roll. So then we know, from what we see in other things, that the particles of water that roll so easily must be round, and must be smooth also.

If the particles of water were large enough for us to see them, they would look to us, on the surface of still water, as a level layer of little shot or round beads, and we should see them rolling about among each other whenever there is the least motion of the water; but, as we can not see the particles, the surface of the water looks like smooth glass when they are all still.

As water moves so easily, it is almost always in motion. It is moved by the wind, and is raised by it sometimes into very high waves. It runs in the brooks and rivers.

In all its motions the water is always trying to be level; and this is the only reason that water ever runs. Water that is level will not run; it will be still. But, when you disturb this level, it will run till it finds its level again.

I will make this plain to you. Suppose that you have a trough stopped at both ends. Put some water in it as it lies on level ground. The water is level in it, and is quiet. Now raise up one end of the trough a little. The water is at once in motion. Why? Because you have disturbed the level. The water runs from the end that you raise toward the other end. Now hold the trough still a little time with the end raised, and as soon as the water gets its level again, it will be as still as it was before.

Suppose the trough is open at both ends, and water is

running in all the time at the raised end. It will keep running toward the lower end. It will be all the time trying to get on a level, but never can. You see here the reason that water runs in a brook or river. You can think of a brook or a river as a trough with one end a little raised; and the water in it is always, as we may say, running after a level, but never finds it. The sea is to a river as a tub would be to the trough that pours its water into it.

There is often great power in the water of a running stream. It works a great deal of machinery in mills of various kinds; and, if the stream be swollen with heavy rains, the water carries away bridges, houses, etc. It does all this in trying to get on a level. If it all could be made level in some way, as you see it in a bowl or a pond, it would do no such violence.

Sometimes men build a dam across a river. This is for the purpose of turning the water off one side into a canal. The dam stops some of the water running in the river, sometimes all of it. In doing this the water is made about level just above the dam, and so is much more quiet than it is any where else in the river.

Children often build mud dams, and the water that they stop is very still because it is level. When the dams give way, how briskly the water runs to try to get on a level again.

Water is always on the same level in the spout of a coffee-

A SUPPOSED DISCOVERY OF PERPETUAL MOTION.

pot that it is in the pot itself, as represented in the first of these figures. If the coffee-pot be turned up, as seen in the second figure, the level is still preserved. If it be turned up a little more, the liquid in the spout, in trying to be on a level with that in the pot, runs out, as represented in the third figure.

A man once thought that he had discovered a way of keeping up perpetual motion. He thought that he could  make a vessel of such a shape that some water in it would never stop moving. The vessel was to be of the shape that you see here. His idea was, that there was so much more water in the vessel than there was in the spout, that it would press the water in the spout up its whole length, and make it run into the vessel. You can see that, if it would operate in this way, the water would be always in motion—it would be going the rounds by way of the spout all the time. But the difficulty is that it would not operate in this way. After the man made his vessel, he found that the water was only as high in the spout as in the vessel, as you see in the figure. It is just as it is with the spout of the coffee-pot.

In the same way, if an aqueduct pipe extend from a spring, the water will not rise any higher in the pipe than it is in the spring. The pipe is to the spring what the spout is to a coffee-pot. And it makes no difference how long the spout is. The water will stand at the same height in a pipe that extends for miles that it does in one that goes but a little way from the reservoir or fountain. This can be illustrated in a vessel with two pipes, as seen here. The

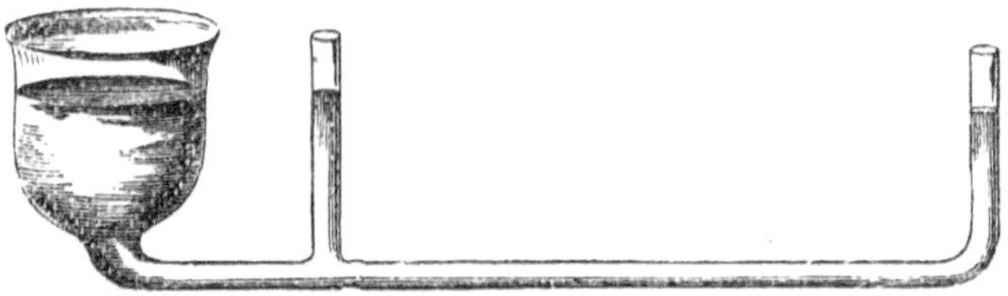

THE PLAYING OF A FOUNTAIN EXPLAINED.

water stands in the branch pipe that is farthest from the vessel at the same height that it does in the near one. Sometimes an aqueduct will supply the lower stories of a building with water, but not the upper stories. The reason is that the upper stories are higher than the level of the water in the fountain from which the water comes.

You have often seen a fountain playing. How beautifully the stream rises and spreads out, dropping in a shower all around! Now why is it that the water rises? It is because the spring from which the water comes is so much higher than the pipe of the fountain. The water in the pipe tries, as we may say, to get on a level with the water in the spring. This I will make plain to you by two figures. In the first figure you see represented a vessel of water, with a pipe extend-

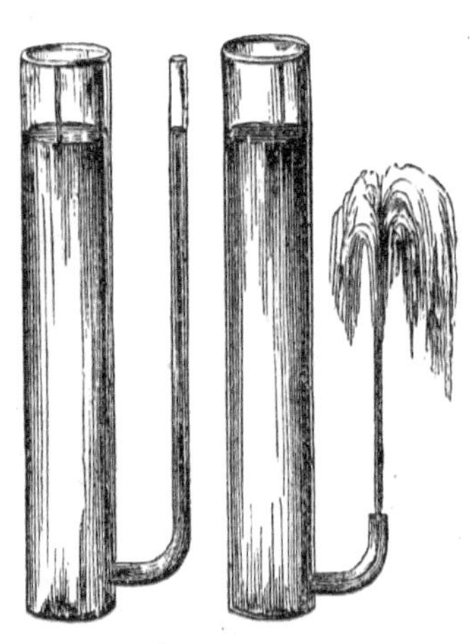

ing from its lower part up at its side. The water stands at the same level in the pipe that it does in the vessel, as in the case of the coffee-pot. Now suppose, as represented in the second figure, the pipe is quite short. If the vessel be filled with water, the water in the pipe, seeking to get to the same level as that in the vessel, will be thrown up in a stream, as you see. The reason that the stream spreads out and drops in a shower is, that the air resists the stream, and so divides it up, because water is so easily separated into parts.

Questions.—*What* is said about water in a bowl? What is said about the particles of water? Give the comparison about shot. Why will not shot run as easily as water from one vessel into another? What is said about the smallness of the particles of water? How do we know that they are round or smooth? If we could see the particles, how would water look to us? What is said about water's being in motion? What makes it run? Tell about water in a trough. Give the comparison about a trough and a river. What is said about the power of running water? What is said about dams? Tell about the level of water in a coffee-pot. Tell about the man's contrivance for perpetual motion. What is said about the pipes of an aqueduct? Why will water sometimes come only to the lower story of a building, and not to the upper? Tell about the playing of water from a fountain. Why does the water come down in a shower of drops?

CHAPTER XVII.

THE PRESSURE OF WATER.

ANY THING that is solid presses only one way, directly down; but water or any fluid presses all ways. It presses just as much sidewise, or even upward, as it does down. The reason is, that the particles of water move about among each other, and are not fastened tight together as they are in a solid. When water freezes, its particles become all fastened together, and then the pressure is all downward.

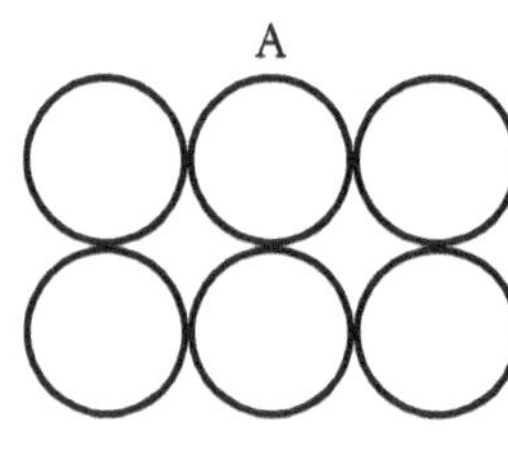

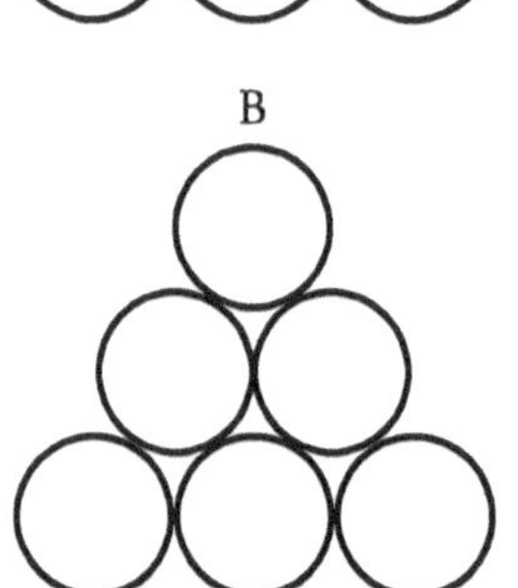

To see how this pressure of the particles of water operates, look at some shot lying together. One shot does not lie right upon another shot below it in this way, *a*, but they lie in this way, *b*. You see that each shot presses down between those that are underneath it. Each shot is trying, as we may say, to get down between its neighbors below; and if there was nothing to prevent it, it would press them apart.

You can see that this is so by trying a little experiment. Put some shot close together on a very smooth surface. Now put another shot on top of them, and you will see that it will press them all apart. If the shot should be rough, and the surface on which you lay them should be rough also, your experiment will not succeed, because the shot will not roll easily. It is for this reason that cannon balls, as you see them piled up in

an ordnance-yard, as represented in the annexed figure, do not roll away. If they were smooth, and the place which they were piled on were smooth, they would all be pressed apart, and the pile would thus be spoiled.

Now see what this sidewise pressure will do in a vessel filled with shot if there should be an opening made in the side. The shot close by the opening will run out, because they are pressed sidewise by the shot lying right above them; and as they go out, those that press them out will be pressed out in their turn by those above them, and so on.

Just so it is with the little fine balls or particles of water. They lie on each other in the same way that shot do. Each particle is pressing always to get down between the particles that are underneath it, as I have showed you it is with the shot. And if you make an opening in the vessel that holds the water, its particles will run, or rather roll out, like the shot, only a great deal easier, because they are so smooth. They are pushed out by this pressing down of each particle between those that are below it.

If you make an opening near the top of a vessel filled with water, it does not run out with much force; but if the opening be made near the bottom, it spouts out as if it was in a great hurry to get out of the vessel. What is the reason of this difference? To understand this, observe that all the particles are pushing downward in the way that I have shown. Those particles, therefore, that are near the bottom, have a great deal more pressure on them than those that are near the top; so that when the opening is made near the bottom, the particles there are pushed out with great force. There is a large crowd of particles pushing down to get out at that opening. And observe, as the water in the vessel lessens, the force of the stream from the opening lessens; it does not leap out so straight as it did at first. It is very much as it is with a crowd pressing through a door. When the crowd is very great, those that are pushed through the door are pushed with great force; but as the crowd lessens, the pressure lessens.

It is found that water runs out of a vessel from an opening in the side close to the bottom just as quickly as it does from an opening of the same size in the bottom itself. What is the reason of this? It is because the little round particles of water roll so easily. They roll out just as easily as they drop out.

See the difference between pressing on a fluid and on a solid. If you press on a block of ice, you press it all one way. If you press it down, you press it all down. If you press it sidewise, it all moves sidewise. And it makes no difference whether your hand, or whatever you push with, covers the whole side of the block or not. But it is not so with water. If you press your hand down into a vessel of water, you press down some of the water, but not all of it. Some of it is pressed up; for, as you press down what is right under your hand, this pushes what is below it off each way to the side, and this pushes up the water that is over it. This is because the round, smooth particles roll so easily on each other. When pressure is made upon them, they roll away from it just where they can—downward, or sidewise, or upward.

There is one way in which you can make all of a body of water go straight along. It must be in a tube, so that it can not escape sidewise, and then there must be something to fit this tube which will push along the water. It must fit exactly, or some of the little particles will slip back by it.

In this way you can push the round body of water in the tube straight along, just as you push a round stick or a long icicle. But suppose that there is a little hole in the tube. This would make no difference if the water were ice, because the particles of a solid are so tightly fastened together; but the pressed liquid, you know, will spout out of the hole, because the particles, not being well fastened together, will escape from the pressure wherever they can. Open a door any where, and out they will leap.

You see the difference between a liquid and a solid in the operation of a squirt-gun, and of one of the stick-guns so common among children. So long as the water is in the squirt-gun, it is all pushed along together, as the stick is in the stick-gun. But as soon as it gets out, it becomes all divided up by the air, just as you saw in the last chapter the water from a fountain does. But the stick, as it flies out of the gun, keeps whole, because its particles are well fastened together. If the water were changed into ice, it would fly out whole as the stick does, for its particles would be so fastened together that the air could not separate them as it does the particles of water.

The difference is still greater between solids and gases. You see this in the firing of a gun or a cannon. The gas into which the powder changes keeps together while it is in the gun, just as the water does in the squirt-gun; but as soon as it gets out, it spreads like the water when it gets out of the squirt-gun, only a great deal more. This is because the particles of the gas are disposed to separate instead of keeping together. They have no attraction for each other; but the ball which the gas drives out of the gun leaves the gas behind it, and goes on whole, because its particles are so well fastened together by attraction.

You see, then, that in a solid there is considerable attraction between the particles; in a fluid there is much less; and in a gas there is none at all.

Questions.—*How* does the pressure of a fluid differ from that of a solid? Give the comparison about shot. Relate the experiment with shot. Tell about the pile of cannon balls. Give the comparison about shot and water running for an opening in a vessel. Why does water run faster from an opening near the bottom of a vessel than from an opening near the top? Why does it run more slowly as the water in the vessel lessens? Give the comparison about a crowd going through a door. Why does water run out from an opening in the side of a vessel close to the bottom as fast as from a hole in the bottom itself? What is the difference between pressing on a solid and pressing on a fluid? How can you make a fluid all go one way in pressing it? What will happen if there be a hole in the tube? Tell about the squirt-gun and the stick-gun. Tell about the ball and the gas in a common gun. Tell about attraction in solids, and fluids, and gases.

CHAPTER XVIII.
ATTRACTION IN SOLIDS AND FLUIDS.

YOU SAW by what I told you in the latter part of the last chapter that the great difference between a solid and a fluid is that the particles of a solid are fastened tightly together, while those of a fluid are not. If you should tie some people tightly together so that they could not move away from each other at all, they would be like the particles of a solid. If you moved them, you would move them all together as you do a stick of wood, a lump of ice, or any thing else that is solid. You can not move them, one one way, and another another way, as you can the particles of water; but if they are all pretty close together, and yet can move about among each other, as you often see in a crowded company, they are like the particles of a fluid. You can make your way among them just as you do among the particles of water when you wade.

But you will ask, Are the particles of a solid really tied together in any way? No; but there is something that does the same thing to them as tying together would. It makes them stick together very tight. We know not what it is, but we call it attraction. We say that the particles of a solid attract each other very much. This is really just what a child would mean by saying that they stick together very close or very tight. Why they thus attract each other, or how they do it, no one has ever yet found out.

It seems to be necessary that the particles should be very near together to attract each other as hard as they do in a solid. If a solid is divided in any way, you know that you can not make the two parts stick close together again. The reason is that you can not bring the particles near enough to each other to hold together. This is commonly so, but not always. If you divide a piece of India-rubber, making a smooth cut with a very sharp knife, you can press the two parts together so as to make them adhere. Boys often try the following experiment: A piece is cut off from two bullets, and each cut place is scraped as smooth as it can be. The two bullets are then pressed together at these smooth surfaces, and they adhere so well that it takes considerable pulling to get them apart. Here enough of the particles on the surfaces are brought near enough together to hold on to each other, or to attract each other, as it is commonly expressed.

The particles of solids, then, attract each other very much, and it is this attraction that makes them solid. But how is it with the particles of liquids? Do they not attract each other? See that drop of water on a window. Why is it in the shape of a drop? If the particles of water did not attract each other they would be spread out on the glass. They would not be in the shape of a drop. They do not attract each other very much, but enough to keep them together in that shape.

But you can spoil that drop very easily. Put your finger on it, and it is gone. It is all spread out now, partly on your finger and partly on the glass. Why is this? It is because the particles attract each other so little that they are easily separated.

Put your finger on a shot, and it remains shot still. Why is it not gone like the round drop of water? Because its particles attract each other so much that they are not easily separated. A mere touch will separate the particles of the drop of water, and make them roll about any way; but you can not do this to the shot without heating it very hot. You can melt it, and then it will be, like the water, a liquid. Its particles now attract each other but little, just as the particles of water do. And then, again, you can freeze the water, and its particles attract each other like the particles of the solid shot.

In some fluids the particles attract each other more strongly than they do in others. And the more they attract each other, the better they keep their drop shape. Pour a very little quicksilver on a flat surface. See the round drops of it roll about! How well they keep their shape! If you touch them you do not spoil them, as you do a drop of water when you touch it. If you break one as you touch it, its parts make only so many little drops or balls. Why is this? It is because the particles of the quicksilver attract each other so much more than the particles of water do. They are so attractive to each other that they are disposed to keep together in little companies.

You sometimes see drops of water on the leaves of plants more round and separate than you see them on window-panes. They roll about like the little balls of quicksilver. See the reason of this. The particles of the drop like each other, as we may say, better than they do the leaf. They are more ready to stick together than they are to stick to the leaf, and so they roll about on it like little balls. As you see the drops on the glass, they are not round, because the particles on one side stick to the glass—that is, they are attracted by it; but the leaf does not attract the particles so much as the glass does, for it lets them keep together in a round form. There is a difference between different leaves about this. On some, the drops of water act as they do on the window-pane, and on others they do as I have just told you; and then, on the same leaves, the drops act differently at different times.

If you pour a little oil on water, you see the oil floating in drops. This is for the same reason that water stands in round drops on some leaves. The water has no attraction for the oil, and so the particles of the oil hold together in little companies on the surface of the water. It is different when oil is spilled upon cloth or wood. It has so much attraction for them that it mingles up with their fibres, instead of forming into round companies as it does on the water.

Whenever there is a little of any liquid by itself, it tends to take a round shape, as seen in the quicksilver, and in the drops of water on windows and leaves. We see a pretty example of this in the manufacture of shot. Perhaps you have seen a shot tower. It is very high. All the shot that are made drop from the top to the bottom. At the top they have the melted lead. They pour it into a sort of cullender—that is, a vessel with holes in it. These holes are quite small. From each one of these holes come out, one after another, drops of the melted lead. Each drop is round. It cools as it goes down all this long distance in the air, and by the time that it gets to the bottom of the tower, it is cold and solid. The shot all fall into a tub of water, so that they may keep their round shape.

Now why is it that the shot are round? Simply because when they begin to fall they are melted lead—that is, a fluid. Their particles are disposed, therefore, to hold together in a round form, like the particles of quicksilver, or of a drop of water.

Bullets are made by pouring the melted lead into moulds.

Think, now, why they can not be made in the same way that shot are. The reason is that there are more particles in a bullet than can hold together in a round shape while the lead is fluid. You can not have very large drops of any fluid. The particles will hold together only in small companies.

There is one thing that you can do with soap-bubbles which perhaps you have never thought of. You can make them roll on a table or on the floor by blowing them along. The reason is that the particles of soap and water mixed together hold on to each other, or attract each other, better than the particles of water alone.

Questions.—*What* is the great difference between a solid and a fluid? Give the comparison about a crowd. Do we know what it is that fastens the particles of a solid together? What is it called? What is said about the particles being near together? Tell about the experiment with the India-rubber and the lead. How do liquids differ from solids in attraction? Why is water on a pane of glass often in drops? Why is it that you can spoil a drop by a touch? Tell how a shot differs from a drop of water. Is the attraction between the particles alike in all fluids? Tell about the quicksilver. Tell about the drops of water on leaves. Tell about oil dropped upon water. How is it with oil spilled upon cloth or wood? Describe shot-making. Why are the shot round? How are bullets made? Why can not they be made in the same way that shot are? What is said about soap-bubbles?

CHAPTER XIX.

WATER IN THE AIR.

I HAVE told you how water is in motion whenever it can be. It runs whenever it can get a chance to do it; but it is in motion in another way, which I will now tell you about.

You hang out a wet cloth to dry. When it is dry, what has become of the water that was in it? It has gone somewhere. Where has it gone? It has flown, like the birds, into the air; but it has gone so quietly that nobody has seen it go. The little fine particles of the water that I have told you about have mixed up with the air, and are blown about with it every where. And so, when you write, as the ink dries on the paper, the water in it flies off into the air, leaving the dark part of the ink behind.

There is a great deal of water that is going up into the air in this way all the time. It goes up from every thing that is wet. After a shower, the ground, the stones, the houses, the trees, and plants are all very wet, but in a little time they are dry again. Most of the water on them has gone up in the air, and is mingled up with it. It has mingled with it in such a way that you can not see it. The air is generally as clear with all this water in it as it is when it is perfectly dry. Even in a bright, clear day, there is a great deal of water mixed up with the air.

But water goes up into the air not merely from things that appear wet. You remember that, in Part First, I told you that water is all the time going out from the pores of the leaves. A great deal of water is furnished to the air in this way.

Then there is water going up from the skins of animals. Much water goes from your skin into the air constantly, even when you can not see that you are perspiring. You can prove this by putting your arm into a glass jar, and holding it there some time. The inside of the jar will become covered with the water that comes from the pores of the skin on your arm. This is like the experiment with leaves noticed on page 77 of Part First.

There is water, too, coming out from the lungs of animals and mixing with the air. It comes from their lungs just as it does from the leaves, which you know are the lungs of plants. You can see this if you breathe upon a cold window. The moisture or water that is breathed out with the air from the lungs gathers upon the glass. In the morning you often see the panes of the windows in your chamber very wet. All this water has come from your lungs as you have slept. In a very cold day the water in your breath freezes upon whatever is about your mouth. You see the water of the breath of a horse frozen on the hairs about his mouth.

So you see water is going up into the air all the time from the ground, the leaves, the animals, and indeed from every thing that is at all moist. It goes up also in great quantities from seas, rivers, lakes, etc. Water, then, is always moving. It runs and it flies. It flies up into the air, and comes down again in the rain to run in the streams. It is ever going its rounds, going up and coming down, and none of it ever stays long in one place. The only way in which it can be made to keep still is to shut it up. Let it be free, and it will soon be gone, either by running or flying.

Commonly the water in the air is not seen, as I have before told you; but sometimes you can see it. You see it in the breath in a very cold day. The cold air makes it look like smoke coming out of the mouth. You see it, too, in the fog. When there is a fog there is a great deal of water in the air. The reason that you can see it is that the particles of water are not as finely divided up as when the air is clear. They are in little companies, as we may say, but there are not enough of them together to make drops. If they were in companies large enough to make drops, they would fall to the ground—that is, we should have a rain.

Sometimes the fog is every where; sometimes it hangs only just over the water. If you are on a very high hill, where you can look off and see a river in the distance, you can sometimes see in the morning a line of fog stretching along where the river is, while it is nowhere else. I once saw a very singular and beautiful scene made by the fog. I had been out on horseback in the night to visit a sick person. As I returned, just before sunrise, I saw from a very high hill a thick fog over all the river below. From the river arose high hills, irregular in their shape, and on the sides of these hills were houses at different heights. The lower houses were all so covered by this dense fog that I could not see them, while those that stood high up on the hills I could see as plainly as ever. It looked as if a sea had come in while I was gone on my visit, and had filled up the valley where the river ran, for the fog rose to the same height on the sides of all the hills. Many of the houses stood upon the very edge of this sea. The scene was so beautiful that I waited to see the sun rise upon it. As it rose, it shone over the tops of the hills, and lighted up this sea of fog, which it in a little time scattered by its heat.

Very thick fogs often hang over large cities, while all around in the country the air may be perfectly clear. London is often covered with such a fog. Sometimes it has been so dense that people could not see to do any business. It is related that the fog over the city of Paris was once so thick that persons who went about with torches often ran against each other, because even lights could not be seen unless they were very near. And in Amsterdam, in a fog in the year 1790, there were over two hundred persons drowned by falling in the darkness into the canals which run through every part of that singular city.

Questions.—*What* becomes of the water when a cloth is dried? Tell about the drying of ink on the paper. Tell about water's going up in the air after a shower. Can you commonly see the water that is in the air? Does water go into the air from things that do not appear wet? What is said about its going from the skins of animals? Tell about the experiment with the glass jar. What is said about water's being breathed out from the lungs? In what ways do you see this shown? What is said about water's being in constant motion? When there is a fog, why is it that you see the water that is in the air? Tell what is said about fogs. Tell about the fogs that hang over large cities.

CHAPTER XX.

CLOUDS.

YOU SEE water in the air in another shape besides fog. You see it in the clouds. A cloud is really fog, but it is high up in the air, while what we commonly call fog is near the ground.

Sometimes rain comes from the clouds, and sometimes they give out no rain. Why is this? When the clouds do not rain, the water in them keeps in the state of fog. The particles are all in small companies; but when the rain comes from the clouds, it is because the cold air makes the particles gather into larger companies, so as to form drops. Then they fall. A mist is different from rain in this way—the companies of particles are not as large as in rain. On the other hand, they are larger than they are in fogs or in clouds.

You remember what I have told you about the gathering of water upon the tumblers in warm weather. It is the coldness of the tumbler that does this. It gathers, or *condenses*, as we commonly say, the water in the air into companies or drops on the tumbler, just as cold air coming upon a cloud condenses the water into drops that fall to the earth in rain.

How swiftly these collections of water, the clouds, are sometimes carried along by the wind! It seems as if they were chasing each other across the sky.

How different are the shapes of the clouds! Sometimes they lie along, stretched out like long straight stripes; and sometimes they are in heaps, piled up one above another.

Then, again, they are spread like feathers. It seems strange that fog high up in the air should collect into such different forms, when near the ground it always appears very much the same.

At morning and evening the clouds are often very beautiful. How do you think that the rich bright colors are made? They are made by the sun shining upon the little companies of water-particles of which the clouds are made. I will tell you more about this when I come to speak of Light.

The clouds are not so high up in the air as most people think they are. Some clouds are higher than others, because they are lighter; and sometimes you can see the clouds that are very high up going in a different direction from those that are nearer to the earth. This is because there are often currents of air very high up that do not go the same way with the winds below. Persons that go up in balloons have found this to be so, as I have before told you.

Clouds are often seen about the sides of high mountains while the sun is shining upon their tops; and persons that are on the top of a mountain may sometimes see clouds below them, while the sky is clear overhead. I was once on the top of Catskill Mountain when a shower passed over. The cloud, after it had passed over the mountain, spread over the country below, so that I looked down upon it. As the cloud was rather a thin one, it was broken into parts. The sun, therefore, shone through the openings here and there; and I remember seeing through one opening in the cloud a beautiful spot, where there was a farm-house and a pond near by, lighted up by the bright sun shining through another opening.

It is the water that goes up from the earth into the air that makes the clouds. I have told you from what a variety of things this water comes. Even the perspiration from your skin and the moisture that is breathed out from your lungs often help to form the clouds that you see floating so high in the air.

As I have told you before, water is ever changing, ever moving. It is silently going up into the air from almost every thing on the earth. Then you see some of it moving along in the clouds. It falls down in the rain. It runs in the brooks and the rivers. In the sea it is lashed into waves by the wind, and is so continually in motion there that the restless sea is a common expression. Water is always going somewhere. Even in places where it seems to be still, it is not so; even there, some of it is all the time going up into the air, and other water comes to take the place of that which goes up.

Water is a great traveler. If any particle of water could write its own history, and tell where it had been ever since it was created, what a varied history it would be! Now it is tossed in the waves; now it is flying off in the air on the wings of the wind; now it is in a cloud; now it falls in a drop from high up in the air; now it sinks into the ground, and is sucked up by some plant; and now, perhaps, from the plant, eaten by some animal, it goes into the blood of that animal. Thus it goes every where and in all sorts of company. Clean as is the draught of water that so refreshes you, it is made up of particles that have been in company with all sorts of things, clean and unclean, in all parts of the earth.

Observe in what very different ways the water takes its start to go off up into the air. Much of it goes up from the ground, and from the surface of lands, and lakes, and seas, and rivers; but a great deal also is sucked up from the ground by the roots of trees and plants, and travels up to the leaves to take its flight into the air from them. And then, too, animals drink water, and eat it in their food, and some of this flies off into the air from their skins and lungs.

The water that goes up in these different ways has also different ways of getting down upon the earth again. That which is high up in the form of clouds comes down in different shapes. When cold air meets the clouds, and changes the water so finely divided in them into drops, it falls in rain. When the air is cold enough to freeze it, it falls in the shape of snow or hail.

Questions.—What is a cloud? Why does it not always rain when it is cloudy? What is the difference between mist and rain? Give the comparison between the rain and the gathering of water on a tumbler. What is said about the shapes of clouds? What about their colors at morning and evening? What is said about the heights of clouds? What about clouds around mountains? Tell about the shower on the Catskill Mountain. What is said about the moisture from your skin and lungs? Tell how the water is always moving and changing. What is said about water as a traveler? Tell in what different ways the water goes up in the air. In what different ways does it come down, and why?

CHAPTER XXI.
SNOW, FROST, AND ICE.

HOW DIFFERENT snow is from water! How white it is as it lies upon the earth like a winding-sheet, covering up the dead leaves and plants! How the wind that makes waves in the water heaps up the snow in drifts! The water slips from your hand as you grasp it, but the snow you can make into hard balls, or roll it up on the ground into larger ones to build snow forts. The snow lies quietly on the sides of hills and mountains, from which, the moment that it melts, it runs down into the valley below.

But, different as the snow is from water, it is nothing but frozen water. It is water made solid; and, as the water becomes solid up in the air before it falls, it forms itself into many different shapes. The snow seems to be all alike as you look at it as it falls. But it is not so. There is variety even here. The snow-flakes have various forms. We can see how different their shapes are if we look at them with a microscope, as they are here represented.

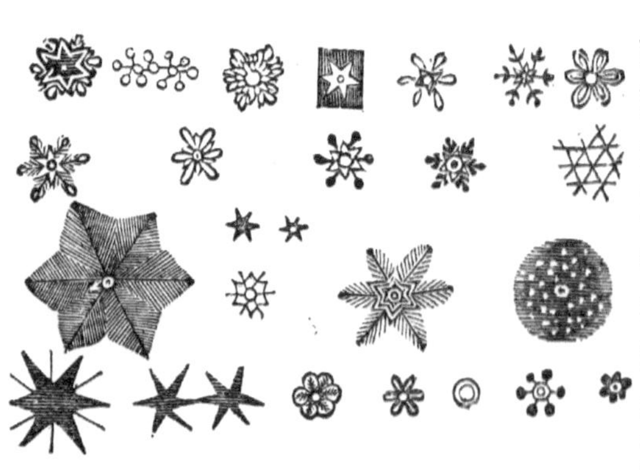

Snow-flakes are beautiful things to look at even with the naked eye. How light, and delicate, and feathery they are! When they are very large and the air is still, how slowly and steadily they fall! Let a few of them light upon your coat sleeve, where you can look at them, and you will admire their beauty; and when we look at them through a microscope, we see that there is not only beauty, but a great variety of beauty in them, as there is in all the other works of God.

Perhaps you have sometimes seen large crystals of quartz or other minerals, and you have admired them because they are so smooth, and regular, and clear. Now every snow-flake is a bundle of little crystals as regular and beautiful as the crystals of quartz. There are millions of these crystals in the snow that you take up in your hand, and in the falling snow they are put together in all the varied forms that you see in the figures above. As I told you about the leaves and the flowers in Part First, so we see, when we examine the snow-flakes, the more we look into the works of God, the more beauty we shall find in them.

How easy it is for God to fill the air with falling crystals, and to pile them up thick on the ground! With a free hand he thus scatters beautiful things in the desolate winter as well as in the blooming summer, and his power is as much seen in the pure crystals of the snow-flake as in the delicate and beautiful structures of the leaf and the flower.

How beautiful is the scene when the snow has fallen gently without wind, and has covered the branches of trees and bushes! Look up into a tree thus covered. There the crystals lie, piled up, like tufts of cotton, out to the very tips of all the branches. Millions and millions of them are on every twig. How many must there be on the whole tree! And how many on all the trees and bushes, and over the whole surface of the ground!

How easily now can God destroy all these crystals! He

can send a warm sun, the wind, or a rain, and they are dissolved and changed into water again. The earth's winter robe, all made of pure white gems, is gone. But God can, whenever he will, turn the clouds above us again into crystals, and strew the earth with them as before.

The great variety of forms which water takes when it becomes solid is often seen on our windows in winter. The figures of the frostwork on them are, you know, almost endless in their variety. These figures are made up of little fine crystals, and these crystals are made out of the water as the cold turns it from a fluid into a solid. How it is that the little particles of water arrange themselves in these clusters of crystals, branching out on the glass in all sorts of shapes, we do not know. God makes them do so in a way that we can not understand. How little do most people think of the wonderful things he is doing before them continually! If they are told that God, with his cold, makes the moisture from their breath into beautiful crystals, they can hardly believe it, and yet they have seen these crystals in the delicate frostwork on their windows winter after winter all their lives.

The figures of this crystal frostwork are often like leaves and flowers, such as we sometimes see on vessels of silver, only much more delicate and beautiful. It is as if God would smile on us in the very frosts of winter as he does in the flowers of summer. In these figures, made of the clustered crystals of the water from our breath, he teaches us, just as he does in the flowers, that he loves to make things beautiful for us to enjoy looking upon them.

The ice, often so very thick, is all crystal. And how beautiful it is when it is formed from clear water in a still place! There is one thing very singular about ice which I must mention. You know that it is lighter than water, for it swims on the top of it instead of sinking in it. This is rather strange. One would suppose that when the fluid water changed into a solid, it would be heavier, because the particles stick tighter together then; but somehow, although they stick together much more tightly, they are farther apart than they were before. It is this that makes the ice lighter. If they were closer together, of course it would be heavier.

We do not understand how God has made this to be so, but we can understand what reason he had for it. It would be very bad to have ice heavier than water. If it were heavier, there would be a great deal of ice on the bottom of our rivers, and ponds, and lakes in the winter. Then it would take a long time for the warm weather to melt this covered-up ice, and in some places it would not all be melted before another winter came. This would make bad work, and every year it would become worse, for there would be additions from year to year to the ice that is not melted. As it is now, the ice is all cleared out of the way in most parts of the world in the early spring, because the sun and the warm rains get at it, and thus the earth becomes ready in a very short time for the summer.

With us the ice and the snow bear rule but a part of the year, but there are regions in the far north where they are always present. No summer comes there to melt them. You have heard of the icebergs in the seas of those regions. These piles of ice often rise like mountains, and many a noble ship has been crushed by them.

There are mountains, too, in some parts of the world so high that winter ever rules on their summits. The ice and the snow are ever there glistening in the sun, even while in the valleys below the golden harvests are ripening in all their beauty.

Questions.—*What* is said about the difference between snow and water? What is snow? Is the snow all alike? What is said about the beauty of snow-flakes? What are snow-flakes? Give the comparison between them and other crystals. What is true of the flakes of snow just as it is of leaves and flowers? What is said about the abundance of the crystals of snow? Tell about the tree covered with snow. What is said about God's destroying the crystals of the snow? What is the frostwork on the windows in winter? What is said about the figures in it? What is ice? What is there very singular about it? What would happen if ice were heavier than water? Tell about the regions where there are always ice and snow. What is true of some mountains?

CHAPTER XXII.

HEAT AND COLD.

W E DO not know what heat is. Wise men have tried to find out what it is, but they have never been able to do it. But we know some things that heat comes from, and some things that it does, and these I will tell you about.

Most of the heat in the world comes from the sun in company with the light. A long way it travels to get here. It is millions and millions of miles that it comes in straight lines to us. Then there is the heat that comes from the fires that we make. Here there is generally light with the heat, just as there is with that which comes from the sun.

Heat and light, when they come together, do not always keep together, but are sometimes separated from each other. If you are standing before a fire and holding a pane of glass before your face, it keeps off the heat—that is, the heat does not come through the glass, or so little of it comes through that you do not feel it. The glass stops the heat, but lets its companion, the light, pass through. Now, if the light of the sun comes through a window, you feel the heat with it. The light and heat come through the glass in company. They are not separated after traveling so many millions of miles together. Why it is different with the fire and the sun we know not. I suppose that the heat and light that come from the sun are in some way more closely united than the heat and light that come from the fire, and therefore are not so easily parted.

But heat is often made without any light. This is the case with the heat of our bodies. There is a sort of burning every where within us to make the heat, but it is a burning without any flame or light. Our bodies are not made warm by fire and clothing, but they keep themselves warm. The only use of our fires and clothing generally is to keep the heat which is made in our bodies from flying off too fast in the air around us. A great deal of heat is made in the bodies of all animals, and the more active they are the more heat they make. You know that when you play very hard you become very much heated. This is because, when the heart beats so quickly, sending the blood all over the body so rapidly, there is more heat manufactured than when the body is still.

Heat is also produced by friction without causing any light. Rub two smooth sticks together, and see how warm they become. The woodwork of machinery has been known to take fire from the heat caused by friction; and Indians used often to kindle their fires by rubbing two sticks together.

You know how easily a match takes fire by rubbing it. This is because there is on the end of it a substance that takes fire with a very little heat, and so requires but a little friction to set it on fire. This curious substance is phosphorus. It is mixed with sulphur on the ends of the matches. When once the phosphorus is set on fire with the friction, it burns the sulphur with it.

It is not many years since the lucifer matches, as they were at first called, were invented. Before this we had a most inconvenient way of getting a light when there was no fire at hand. A flint was struck upon a piece of steel again and again over some tinder. The object was to make a spark which would set fire to the tinder. This was not always readily done, and I remember getting out of patience many a time in working over my tinder-box when I was a student in college.

There is a great deal of heat made inside of the earth, and it is supposed by some that all the middle of this great round ball that is called the earth is an immense fire like a furnace. The earthquakes are supposed to be caused by the heavings of this fire, and the volcanoes are so many chimneys where the fire of this great furnace gets vent.

Heat is a thing, but there is really no such thing as cold. Any thing is cold when there is but little heat in it. Whether all the heat can get out of any thing we do not know. There is heat even in ice. This has been proved in this way: Two pieces of ice were rubbed together in a very cold day, and some of the ice became melted. How was this? The air all about the ice was too cold to melt it; and it must be, therefore, that it was the heat in the ice, waked up, as we may say, and brought out by the rubbing, that melted the ice.

What feels cold to you may feel warm to another. If, when your hand is very warm, you take hold of some one's hand that is only moderately warm, it will feel cool to you, and perhaps even cold; but if some one whose hands are quite cold takes hold of the same hand, it will feel to him quite warm.

Try a little experiment, which will show the same thing in another way. Take three vessels. Put into one water as hot as your hand can bear, into another ice-cold water, and into the third water that is a little warm, or that has had the chill taken off. Now put one of your hands into the vessel of hot water, and the other into the vessel of cold water. Keep them there a little while. Then take them out, and put both into the vessel that has the water which is slightly warmed. The water in this will feel cold to the hand which was in the hot water, and warm to the hand which was in the cold water.

For the same reason, water standing in a room will feel quite warm to you if you have been handling snow, though it is cold to others. So, also, water that was very cold to you before eating ice-cream, seems, after eating it, to have lost all its coldness.

So you see that heat and cold are not two things separate from each other, of which you can tell where one begins and the other ends. It is convenient to speak of the cold as if it were a thing, just as heat is, though, as I have told you, it is not; and it is well enough to do so if we understand the matter right.

Questions.—*What* do we know about heat? From what does most of the heat come? What does it come with? What is said about sun-heat and fire-heat? Tell about the making of heat in our bodies. What is the use of our fires and clothing in cold weather? Why do you become so much heated on playing hard? What is said about friction? Explain the operation of Lucifer matches. What is said about tinder-boxes? What is said about the inside of the earth? When is any thing cold? Is there any thing that has no heat in it? How is it proved that there is heat in ice? Does what feels cold to one always feel cold to another? Give the experiment of the three vessels of water. What other things can be explained in the same way?

CHAPTER XXIII.

THE DIFFUSION OF HEAT.

H EAT ALWAYS tries to spread itself in all directions. If you put the end of a poker in the fire and hold it there, you do something more than heat that end. You heat the whole of it up to the end that you hold in your hand. The reason is, that the heat that comes into the end of the poker which is in the fire spreads through all of it to the other end.

 This figure represents an experiment that you can try, which shows how the heat spreads through any thing solid. A rod or bar of iron is taken, and small balls of wood are fastened to it, as you see, by some wax. Now, on heating one end of the bar with a lamp, as the heat spreads along the bar, the balls one after another drop off, because the wax that holds them melts.

Heat spreads from one thing to another when it can get a chance to do it. If one thing that has a good deal of heat in it touches or is near by another that has less heat in it, it parts with some of its heat, and lets it go into the other thing, and after a little while one will be as warm as the other. For this reason, in a warmed room, all the furniture, the tables, the bureaus, the carpet, and the walls of the room become heated alike. The heat from the fire spreads through them all. It takes some time to do this, but it is done.

It is because heat goes from one thing to another that ice

melts in warm water or warm air. Some of the heat in the water or air goes into the ice and melts it, and the melting ice cools the water or air by thus taking a part of its heat.

The heat which I have told you is made in our bodies spreads continually in the air around us. This is the reason that a room which is comfortably warm becomes uncomfortably so when a large company has been in it for a little time. A great deal of heat spreads into the air from so many bodies.

Did you ever think how fanning cools you? It is by making the heat go off faster from your body into the air. It moves off the air that has become heated by your body, and brings some other air to take its place. For the same reason, blowing upon any thing that is hot helps to cool it. It brings the air to it faster than it would come without the blowing, and so the heat passes off faster. But perhaps you will ask me to explain why it is that blowing on your fingers when they are cold warms them, when blowing on any thing hot cools it. This is plain enough. The air that you blow on to your fingers is warmer than they are, and gives some of its heat to them. If, on the contrary, your fingers were hot with fever, blowing on them would cool them, for they would then give some of their heat to the air that is cooler than they are.

Heat spreads through some things more easily than it does through others. It spreads through iron very easily indeed, as you know by holding an iron poker with one end in the fire, but it does not spread any thing like as easily through wood. If you hold a stick of wood with one end in the fire, you can let it burn off without feeling the heat at the other end; but you could not hold a poker so long in the fire, for the heat would spread to the end in your hand so much that it would soon be too hot for you to hold it. So iron is said to be a better *conductor* of heat than wood, for the heat is conducted through it more easily than through the wood.

It is for this reason that wooden handles are put upon some iron tools that are used in operations about the fire. The tool which the tinman uses in soldering has a wooden handle. If it had not, his hand would be burned by the heat going up to it by the iron handle; but very little of it goes into the wooden handle and spreads there, because wood is so poor a conductor of heat. We do not need wooden handles for tongs and pokers, because we do not have to keep them in the fire so long as the tinman does his soldering-iron. The handle of a metallic tea-pot is, you know, made of wood; for, if it was metallic, the heat from the tea would spread through it, and make it so hot that it could not be held in the hand. The holder which is used in ironing is of service, because it is so poor a conductor of heat. The heat does not readily go through it to the hand; so, also, we sometimes use paper to take up things that are hot, because the paper, being a poor conductor, does not let much of the heat pass through it to the hand. You have seen people wrap up ice in flannel to keep it from melting. The flannel here does for the ice what the woolen or paper holder does for the

EXPERIMENT ON A STOVE.

hand—it prevents the heat in the air around from getting to the ice.

Here is represented an experiment which shows how heat spreads through different things with different degrees of rapidity. Some pieces of different things of the same size and shape are put on top of a stove. They are pieces of iron zinc, copper, lead, marble, and brick. On the top of each is put a little bit of wax. The wax on the copper melts first, because this is a better conductor of heat than any of the others. Next is the iron; next, the zinc; next, the lead; next, the marble; and last of all, the brick.

In air that is kept still heat spreads very slowly; but heat, when it can, always sets air in motion. I have told you, in Chapter XIII., how heated air rises and cold air takes its place. This is going on all the time about a stove. As fast as the air is heated, it goes up by the stove and the pipe, and cold air keeps coming to the stove to be heated. In this way all the air in the room is, after a little while, warmed. Now, if the air could all be kept still instead of being kept in motion in this way, it would take a long time for the heat to be spread from the stove through it, for air, like wood, is a poor conductor of heat.

We see the fact that confined air is a poor conductor of heat in a great many things. Some of them I will mention. You have sometimes seen double windows. It is the confined air between the outer and the inner windows that prevents the heat of the air in the room from spreading to the air out doors. When the window is single, the outside air cools the air in the room through the window in this way: The air in the room close to the window gives some of its heat to the glass, and, being thus cooled, it falls, and some more warm air comes to be cooled in like manner, and then falls, and so on continually. All this time the cold air on the outside keeps coming to get warmed by the glass, and as it is warmed it goes up, and more cold air comes to take its place. But all this is pretty much prevented where the windows are double, by the confined air between them.

There is a great deal of air in snow. This is the chief reason that snow is so apt to keep the ground from being frozen. It is the earth's winter coat of confined air, for there is air mingled with its flakes as they are piled upon each other on the ground. Last spring I picked up a pear in my garden that was as fresh as it was when it fell upon the ground in the fall. It happened to lie in a spot where the snow lay all the winter, and was thus kept from freezing.

Furs are commonly spoken of as if they had some warmth in them. This is a mistake. They are not warm of themselves. They only serve to keep in the heat that is made in the body, and they do this by the air that is mingled up with the fibres of the fur. This confined air is a poor conductor, and so the heat made in the body does not readily pass off through it into the air around. Fur is therefore to an animal, in this respect, what snow is to the ground, or what double windows are to a room; and the finer the fur is, the better does it keep the heat in, because the air is more confined among fine fibres than it is in coarse hair. And it is curious, that if an animal with thick fur is taken from the cold country where he belongs to a warm climate, and kept there, his fur gradually loses its fineness and thickness, and becomes like hair. This is because he does not need his thick, furry coat where the weather is warm.

You remember that I told you in Part First that inside of the covering with which every one of the buds on the trees is protected from the cold of winter there is a fine down. This, I told you, was the bud's little blanket. You can understand, now, how this keeps it from being chilled by the wintry blasts. It is the air that is confined between the fibres of this downy blanket that does it.

You remember, also, that I told you in Part First about tying straw around trees to protect them from the winter's cold. Now you know that every stalk of straw is hollow, and so is full of air, and it is the air in all the stalks of the straw that makes it so good a coat for the trees. This coat protects them just in the same way, then, that an animal is protected by its furry coat, or the bud by its blanket of down.

Questions.—*What* is said of the spreading of heat? What is said about its going from one thing to another? How is ice melted? What is said about heat's spreading from our bodies? Tell how fanning cools you. Why does blowing a hot thing help to cool it? Why does blowing upon cold fingers warm them? Explain what is meant when we say that some things are better conductors of heat than others. Give the illustrations. How does heat commonly spread in air? How would it be if the air could be kept still? Explain how double windows keep the heat in. What is said about snow? What about furs? Why does a fine fur keep the heat in better than a coarse one? How does taking an animal to a warm climate affect the fur? Tell about the blankets of the buds. Tell about covering trees with straw.

CHAPTER XXIV.
WHAT HEAT DOES.

HEAT MAKES most things larger, or *expands* them, as it is commonly expressed. I will give you some examples of this.

I have already told you in Chapter XIII. how heat expands air. You remember the two experiments with the bladder before the fire. You remember also what I told you about the expansion of the air in apples and chestnuts by heat.

EXPERIMENT SHOWING HOW AIR IS EXPANDED BY HEAT.

Here is represented another experiment which shows that heat expands air. A glass tube, with a bulb on the end of it, is put with its open end into a tumbler of water. Of course the tube is full of air. Now, on putting the warm hand on the bulb, as represented, the air in it will be warmed. The air, therefore, swells, and there is not room for it all in the tube; and so some of it escapes in bubbles, as you see, through the water.

The snapping wood, you know, often throws out sparks. These are parts of the wood partly burned that happen to be right on the spot where the confined heated air was that has broken loose. The more porous wood is, the more apt it is to snap. The solid walnut seldom snaps; but the chestnut, which is very porous, is always snapping. So, too, dry wood snaps more than green, because the sap has dried up, and air has taken its place in the pipes of the wood.

Air expanded by heat, as you have before seen, always rises. It is pushed up, as I have already told you, by the colder air, which is heavier. This keeps the air always moving. It is never still, for heat is always acting upon it. Even when it is so still that we say there is no wind, it is not perfectly still. There is all the time the going up of warm air and the coming down of that which is colder. You can see this in a room if you shut it up so as to make it quite dark, and let only a little light in by partly opening one shutter. Though the air seems to you to be perfectly still, you will see, where this light is let in, little motes flying up and down. This is because there are currents in the air, and these are made by heat.

It is heat that puts the air in motion so as to produce winds. You have heard people talk about the cool, refreshing sea breeze. This comes up commonly in the afternoon. It is caused in this way: The earth becomes very much heated by the hot sun during the day, and so heats the air above it. This heated air rises, and the air which comes off from the cool water to take its place makes the sea breeze.

You see why it is that heated air is lighter than cold air. It is swelled by the heat without having any thing added to it. Its particles are put farther apart. It is made thinner, and air, as it becomes cold, is contracted or made smaller. Its particles are brought closer together, and so it is made thicker and heavier.

And so it is with water or any liquid. When it is heated

it becomes larger and thinner, just as air does, and so is lighter. It rises, therefore, being pushed up by the heavier cold water. There are, therefore, the same up and down currents in water that there are in the air. When one is heating water, the warm water is all the time going up, and the cold water is going down. If you heat it in a glass vessel, and have some little light things in the water, you can see them go up and down in the currents in the same way that you see motes moving up and down in the currents of the air.

The grocer knows very well that heat expands all liquids. His molasses and oil are much thinner, and so run more freely in summer than in winter. And the gallon of molasses or oil that you buy in summer does not weigh so much as the same quantity in winter, for the same reason that heated air is lighter than cold air.

In the thermometer you see the expansion or swelling of a fluid by heat. Put your finger on the bulb, and hold it there a little while. The mercury rises, you see. What is the reason? The warmth of your finger swells or expands the mercury, and it rises, because it needs more room. You can do the same thing by breathing on it. Your warm breath will expand the mercury. This is just what the warm air does to it; and when the weather is cold, the cold air shrinks or contracts it. When it is very cold indeed, the mercury is very low down in the tube, because it is so much contracted by the cold air; and when it is hot weather, the mercury is very high, because it is so much swollen by the heat. You can understand, by what I have told you, how it is that we judge of the heat of the air by the thermometer.

Heat expands solid substances, though not as much as it does the air, and gases, and liquids. If a rod of iron will just go through a hole in another piece of iron, you can not get it into that hole when the rod is heated, because it is swollen or expanded by the heat. The tire of a wheel is heated when it is put on the wheel. Why this is done I will explain to you. The tire is made a little too small for the wheel. You can not put it on the wheel while it is cool, but when it is heated it goes on very easily, because the heat has made it larger. Cold water is now poured upon it, and as it contracts it fits very tightly, giving great firmness to the wheel. It could not be made to fit so tightly in any other way.

So I have showed you how heat expands various things. It sometimes does more than this when there is enough of it. It changes a solid into a fluid. For example, it changes ice into water. So it makes the hard iron into a fluid so that you can pour it like water, as you can see in an iron foundry when the workmen are casting. It takes more heat to melt iron than it does to melt ice, and it takes more to melt ice than to melt mercury. It takes so little to melt mercury that we can seldom get a chance to see it solid. In some of the coldest regions of the earth, however, it is often seen solid.

But heat does more than this. It changes some liquids into something like air or gas. For example, it changes water into steam. There must be a great deal of the heat to do this—much more than is required to change ice into water.

I have told you in Parts First and Second much about what heat does to life in vegetables and animals. The heat of spring wakes up the seeds and the buds; and stalks, and leaves, and flowers, and fruits come forth from them, mak-ing the earth cheerful and gay. It wakes up, too, multitudes of animals, that with their moving about and their various voices make the world every where so busy. Thus, almost like magic, does heat work in the animal and vegetable world. I know not any thing in which the effects of heat are so wonderful as in the egg. Look at a hen's egg as it is opened, and see the golden yolk in the midst of the pure, glairy white. It does not seem that this could be changed into a chicken, with its bones, and muscles, and nerves, and feathers, and claws, and by nothing but heat; but so it is. The hen has only to keep the egg warm by sitting on it, and all this happens; and the chicken, when it is all formed, bursts the shell, and comes out from its round white prison.

Questions.—How does heat affect most things? Explain the snapping of wood on the fire. What are the sparks that are thrown out? What kinds of wood snap most? What keeps air moving, and how? How can you know that air is not still when it seems to be? What makes the wind? What is said about the sea breeze? Why is heated air lighter than cold air? How is it with water? What is said about heating water? What effect does heat have on molasses and oil? Explain the operation of the thermometer. What is said about the expansion of solids by heat? Give the experiment of the rod of iron. Explain the putting of a tire on a wheel. What is said about the changing of solids into fluids by heat? What change does very great heat produce in water? What does heat do in the animal and the vegetable world? What is said about the egg?

CHAPTER XXV.
STEAM.

STEAM IS like air in three things. It is very thin; it is very elastic, or has a great deal of springiness; and you can not see it. Now perhaps you will say that this last is not true, and that we often see steam puffing out of a steam-engine or out of a tea-kettle; but this that we see is not really steam. It is not like the steam that is in the boiler of the engine or in the tea-kettle. It is a cloud of fog that the steam has turned into on coming out into the air. It is just like common fog, except that it is hot. Real steam you can not see as you see this.

Perhaps you will ask how I know that we can not see steam, as I can not look into a boiler or a tea-kettle. If we boil water in a glass vessel, we can see the steam if it can be seen; but we see nothing in the vessel over the water, and yet we know that there is a plenty of steam there, for the steam-fog is made in the air by the steam coming out at the mouth of the vessel.

But we do not need this proof to show us that steam can not be seen. Look at the nose of a tea-kettle when the water is boiling in it quite briskly. Close to it, for half an inch or more, you can not see the steam-fog at all. What is the reason? There is a stream of steam coming out as fast as it can get out, but the air has not yet had a chance to change it into fog. It must spread out a little first. When it begins to spread out, the cool air makes the particles of steam form into companies, and it is a multitude of these companies that you see in the cloud of steam, as it is called, that comes from a steam-engine or from a tea-kettle. The air really changes the steam into water, for fog, as I have told you in Chapter XIX., is water in companies that are too small to make drops.

See, now, how steam is made out of the water in a tea-kettle. The fire heats the water that is nearest to it in the kettle. This rises, and more water comes to take its place and be heated, and so the water keeps circulating up and down, the warmer going up and the cooler going down. After a while, when the water all gets to be very hot, you hear a simmering noise. Now the steam begins to be made. The sound is made by little bubbles of steam which are formed at the bottom of the kettle. Soon larger bubbles of steam are made, because so much more of the water becomes hot enough to be readily made into steam; and the rising of these bubbles makes a great commotion, as you can see if the water be in an open pot. All this process of steam-making you can see if the water is boiled in a thin glass bottle, or flask, as it is called.

There is a great deal of force in steam. It is steam that works the locomotive, and moves along the great steamship in the water. Sometimes it shows its power in destruction, as when it bursts a boiler.

Now what is it that makes steam so powerful? To understand this, look at a locomotive when it is standing still, with its boiler full of steam. A valve is opened, and out rushes the steam, spreading itself, and turning into a cloud of fog. It is this trying to spread itself that makes the steam so powerful. If the valve were not opened the boiler might explode; for, as the steam is not used as it is while the locomotive is going, there would be more and more of it in the boiler, for it is making all the time. The force with which it rushes out when the valve is opened shows how much power it exerts in trying to spread itself.

You see the same thing in the rattling of the lid of a tea-kettle when the water is boiling in it. The steam which is made has not room in the kettle to spread itself. It gets out, therefore, wherever it can. It blows out at the nose; and if the water boils very briskly, it can not get out fast enough at the nose, and so it keeps lifting the lid and puffing out there.

When the steam is shut up very tightly, as it is in the boiler of a steam-engine, it has very great power, and the more steam there is thus shut up the greater is the power. Men are sometimes careless about this, and get so much steam made in the boiler that it bursts. This is just as the roasted chestnut is burst by the steam and heated air that are in it. The boiler bears the pressure of the steam as long as it can. This pressure is made by the steam's trying to spread itself, or by its expansive force, as it is expressed. After a while, the steam being made all the time, and being crowded together, as we may say, the boiler all at once gives way with a loud noise. The noise is caused in the same way as the pop of the roasted chestnut. It is the sudden shaking that the escaping steam gives to the air.

There is always a safety-valve to a steam-engine. This is commonly kept shut by a weight which is upon it. But when there comes to be a great deal of steam in the boiler, it has expansive power enough to raise the valve, and so some of the steam escapes. This prevents the boiler from bursting, and hence the valve is called a safety-valve. Now, if there happen to be a weak place in the boiler, and the weight on the valve is heavier than it should be, the weak place will be apt to give way rather than the valve, and an explosion results. Many a boiler is burst in this way.

I have told you about another way in which boilers are burst in the chapter on Powder. It is this. The boiler is carelessly left to get nearly empty, and the fire therefore makes it very hot. Then, when more water is let into it, a great deal of steam is made all at once. This exerts its expansive force with such violence that the boiler gives way. You can understand how this is if you see a little water dropped upon red-hot iron. A great cloud of steam arises, spreading itself in the air, and you can see that if this were pent up it would make a strong pressure in trying to get free.

A boy was once much surprised to see the melted lead which he poured into a piece of elder, from which he had scooped the pith, thrown with great force against the ceiling. The reason was, that the elder was moist, and the moisture inside being changed all at once into steam, the expansive force of the steam threw out the lead, just as the expansive force of the gas made all at once from powder throws the ball out of a gun.

It takes but a little water to make a good deal of steam, and this explains an explosion that once occurred in a cannon foundry in London. There happened to be some water in one of the moulds, and, therefore, when the melted metal was put into it, this water was at once made into steam, and this, in trying to get free, made such an explosion as to blow up the whole foundry. Perhaps you can hardly believe that so little water could do so much when turned suddenly into steam. But you must remember that the steam occupies, if set free, about 1700 times as much room as the water does from which it is made. It tries to get this room, and in doing this it exerts great force, especially if it be made very suddenly.

You will like to know how the sound of the steam-whistle is made. In the chapter on the hearing, in Part Second, I told you that sound is always caused by the vibration or shaking of something. Now in the steam-whistle there is a sort of bell-shaped thing with a thin edge or rim. The steam, as it is let out through the whistle, strikes against this rim, and makes it vibrate, and so produces the sound. The sound is very loud, because the steam comes out with great force.

Questions.—*In* what three respects is steam like air? Tell about the steam-fog. How do we know that steam can not be seen? What is said about the steam that comes from the nose of a tea-kettle? Describe how steam is made. In what way can you see the whole process? What is said about the force of steam? How is its force shown in the locomotive when it is stopped at a station? Tell about the rattling of the lid of a boiling tea-kettle. Explain how boilers are commonly burst. How does the safety-valve operate? How is it that the safety-valve does not always keep boilers from bursting? What other way in which boilers are burst is mentioned? Tell about the accident with the melted lead. Tell about the blowing up of an iron foundry. How is the sound of the steam-whistle made?

CHAPTER XXVI.

LIGHT.

As I told you about heat, that we do not know what it is, so, also, we do not know what light is. But we know many things about light, just as we do about heat.

The chief use of light is to enable us and different animals to see. I have told you something about seeing in Part Second. It is the light entering the eye that makes us see. When we see the sun, or the flame of a candle, or a flash of lightning, the light which is made by these different things goes into the eye, and so we see them.

These things that I have mentioned make light, and some of this light comes directly to our eyes. But we see things that do not make any light. No light is made by the houses, and trees, and persons, and many other things that we see about us. How is it that we see them? It is in this way: The light that shines on them bounds off from them and goes into our eyes. Thus, if you see a tree, the light strikes upon it, and then bounds from it into your eyes, and makes a picture or image there of the tree. When the light bounds off in this way, it is said to be *reflected*.

There is a great deal of this reflection of light. It is often reflected more than once, sometimes many times. Thus, if you see a tree in a looking-glass, the light is reflected twice. First, it bounds off or is reflected from the tree, and then it is reflected from the glass to your eyes. So if you look at your own face, the light first strikes your face, and is reflected from it to the glass; and then it is reflected from the glass to your eyes, and pictures the image of your face there.

Now observe that the light that is reflected from your face makes an image or picture of it in the glass. It is precisely such an image that the light entering your eye makes in the back part of it, on a thin sheet or membrane that is there, except that it is a much smaller image.

Every thing reflects light, but some things reflect it more than others. Rough things do not reflect as much as smooth things. How perfectly the smooth water of a pond reflects the houses and trees at its side when there is no wind! You know that all polished surfaces shine. This is because they reflect a great deal of light.

It is a reflected light that comes to us from the moon and from some of the stars. The light goes to them from the sun, and then is reflected from them. They are said, therefore, to shine by a borrowed light. The reason that we can not see the stars in the daytime is, that the light from the sun is so much brighter than their light. The moon shines so much more brightly than the stars, that we can see it in the daytime when it is above the horizon, though the greater brightness of the sun makes it quite faint.

I have told you that light is sometimes reflected more than twice, even many times. When you look at a person in a room into which the sun is not directly shining, where does the light by which you see him come from? It is not the light that comes straight from the sun, for this is not shining upon him. It is the light reflected from things around him. This reflected light strikes upon him, and is thus again reflected from him, and some of it enters your eyes, enabling you to see him.

Light is thus reflected back and forth from one thing

to another; and a great deal of light is reflected from every thing all the time, and in all directions. Suppose a great assembly are all looking at one person. The light is reflected from him, and goes into a thousand eyes at once in all parts of the house, making a picture of him in all of them. What a wonderful painter light is! How many pictures it is making all the time in the eyes of men and animals, and on mirrors and all smooth things every where!

Another use of light is to make plants and animals grow. I have told you in Part I. how plants turn toward the light, as if they loved it. It really has a great deal to do with their growth.

This is very plain whenever we see a plant that has grown in the dark. It looks pale and sickly. A good deal of light is needed as really as a free circulation of air to make plants healthy and strong; and the same is true of animals. People that live in dark, under-ground rooms in cities are injured by the want of light as well as by the want of good air.

Most of the light in the world comes from the sun. It comes from there with the heat, as I have before told you. They travel in company. It is a very long journey. It is many millions of miles. The light is a little more than eight minutes coming from the sun to the earth.

Light travels very fast. It travels faster than sound does. You see a man cutting wood a considerable distance off, and you hear the sound of each blow of his axe a little after you see it. The reason is that the light comes from him to your eye quicker than the sound comes to your ear. You see a cannon fired at a distance; you first see the flash, and then afterward hear the report. The thunder comes generally some time after the flash that causes it; that is, the light of the flash gets to your eye some time before the sound of it reaches your ear. By observing, it has been found out just how fast sound and light travel; and so, by looking at a watch in a thunder-storm, we can tell how far off the lightning is.

Light, besides traveling faster than sound, can travel a great deal farther. Lightning may be so far off that you can not hear the thunder. The light reaches your eye, but the sound dies away before it reaches your ear.

Most of our light, I have said, comes from the sun; but much light comes from burning substances—burning wood, coal, oil, tallow, gas, &c.

Light is made by some animals. The glow-worm gives out a soft and beautiful light. The fire-fly sparkles as it flies about in the evening. In Cuba and in South America ladies wear in their hair as ornaments, in evening parties, some small insects that give a very brilliant light. Sometimes the sea sparkles beautifully with light, which is made by multitudes of very little animals in it. We see this light often in the wake of a vessel, or behind the wheel of the steamer, or in the water that falls from the lifted oar. It is when the water is disturbed in some way that these animals make their light. There are some flowers in very warm countries that shine in the night. You have seen what is called light-wood. This is decayed wood, and it is something in the decay that makes the light. Light is also sometimes given out by animal substances that are decaying. It is most often seen in putrid fish.

It is supposed that in all these cases the light is made by phosphorus, the same substance that lights so easily in the Lucifer match. This curious substance is commonly kept in water. If a stick of it be taken out of the water in the evening, it appears lighted like a glow-worm; and if

you rub it upon any thing, the streaks of it will give a brilliant white light. Sometimes, on rubbing a match, if it does
not take fire, you see for a little time lighted streaks where
you rubbed it. This is caused by the phosphorus rubbed
off from the match. When the match burns, you do not
see these lighted streaks, for the same reason that you do
not see the stars when the sun shines.

Questions.—What is the chief use of light? How do we see? How
do we see things that do not make light? How do we see things in a
mirror? How is the image in the mirror like that in the eye? What
difference is there in things in reflecting light? What is said about
the light of the moon and the stars? Why can not we see the stars
in the daytime? Why can we see the moon in the daytime? What is
mentioned which shows that light is often reflected many times before
it comes into the eye? Tell what is said about an assembly all looking
at a speaker. What effect has light upon plants and animals? What
is said about living in dark rooms? How long is light in coming from
the sun? Give some examples which show that it travels faster than
sound. Can sound go as far as light? From what besides the sun does
light come? Tell about the fire-flies—the sparkling that we often see
in the sea—light-wood. What is said about phosphorus?

CHAPTER XXVII.

COLOR.

THE LIGHT that comes from the sun is, you know, a white light. Now in this white light are the different colors of the rainbow. Indeed, it is these colors mixed together that make the white color of the sun's light. This was proved by Sir Isaac Newton in this way: He had a hole in a shutter through which he let a very little of the sun's light into a dark room. He had a screen for it to strike upon, and on this it made a bright white spot. He then let it shine through a three-cornered piece of glass, called a prism. This turned the ray of light out of its way, and made it shine upon another part of the screen; and, besides this, the spot of light on the screen, instead of being round, as it was before, was now lengthened out, and had seven different colors in it.

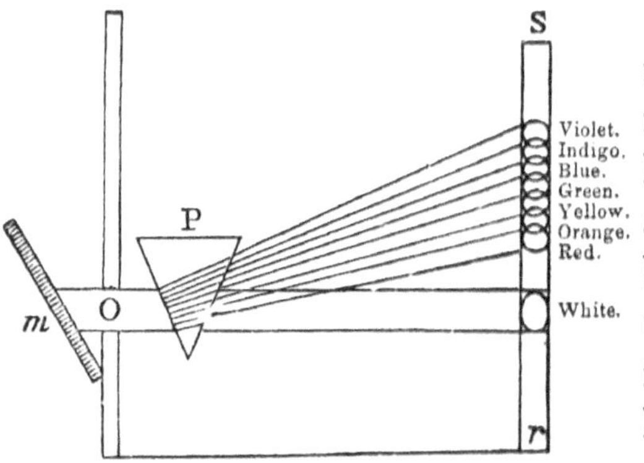

All this is represented on this figure. At O is the hole in the shutter, and *m* is a mirror by which a little of the bright sunlight is thrown into this hole. Without the prism it would go straight to the screen, S *r*, and make a round white spot where the word *white* is. But with the prism, P, the beam of light is turned out of its straight path, and is divided into the different colors as marked in the figure. The reason that these colors are seen so distinct from each other is, that they are bent out of their way in different degrees—the orange a little more than the red, the yellow a little more than the orange, and so on, the violet being most bent of all. You see this represented on the figure.

This and various other experiments, tried by Newton and others, show that the white light of the sun is not a simple thing. It can be cut up, as we may say, into different parts. The glass prism does this. You have often seen it done without thinking much about it. You have seen it done by ice. When there has been a rain, and the rain, as it fell, froze upon the branches of the trees, and the wind and the sun have together broken the ice on the trees, and strewed the ground with it, you have seen these pieces of the ice brilliant with all the colors into which they have divided the bright light of the sun. It seemed as if the ground was covered with gems of every hue; and as you looked up into the tree, it seemed to you that every twig also was strung with gems.

You see the same thing in the rainbow. The white light of the sun is separated by the drops of rain into its different colors just as is done by the glass prism, and thus the bow is made. Exactly how this is done you are not old enough yet to understand. What you see in the rainbow and in the scattered pieces of ice you can also sometimes see in the dew-drops in the morning. They sparkle with all the different colors. The grass seems to be filled with gems of every variety. The drops of dew do this by dividing up the sunlight, as the drops of rain do when the rainbow is made.

Now see how it is that different things have different colors. When a thing is white it is because all the different parts or colors of the light are reflected from it to our eyes.

On the other hand, when a thing is perfectly black, it is because none of the colors are reflected. Black is, then, no color at all, while in white all the colors are mixed together.

Newton proved that white is a mixture of all colors in a very pretty way. He made a wheel, on the edge of which he painted all the seven colors. When he whirled it round very fast indeed he could not see the colors separate from each other. The colors all went to his eye mixed up together, and being mixed, they made a white color, just as they do in a beam of light. The rim of the wheel then looked to him as if it was white.

He proved the same thing in another way. He took powders of these seven different colors, and ground them together very finely. The colors all disappeared. The mixed powder was almost white. It would have been entirely white if he could have mixed the powders as thoroughly as the colors are mixed by the Creator in the light of the sun.

But I have not yet told you how one thing looks green, another yellow, another blue, etc. I have only told you why one thing is black and another white. When a thing looks blue, it is because none but the blue part of the light is reflected to your eye. All the rest of the colors stop right there in the thing. They do not bound off from it as the blue does. So, when a thing is green, the green part of the light is reflected to your eye. When a thing is orange color, the orange part of the light is reflected, and so on.

If you have pieces of glass, and let the light come through them, you see the same thing in another way. Light coming through blue glass comes to your eye blue, because all the other colors stop in the glass, while the blue passes on; and light coming through green glass is green for the same reason.

Now what is done with the colors that stay in things that they come to we do not know. If a thing looks blue, only one color out of the whole seven in the light is thrown off from it. The other six colors, red, orange, yellow, green, indigo, and violet, stop right there in the thing. What it does with them is a mystery. It puts them out of sight in some way, and sends only one of the seven colors to our eyes.

Questions.—*What* makes the color of the sun's light white? How many colors are there in a ray of the sun? Mention Sir Isaac Newton's experiment. Tell what is represented by the figure. What does the glass prism do to the light? Tell about the colors of the scattered ice. How is the rainbow formed? Tell about the colors in the dew. When is a thing white? When is a thing black? Tell about Newton's painted wheel. Tell about his mixture of powders. Explain how it is that one thing is blue, another green, another yellow, etc. How is it when light comes through things, as colored pieces of glass? What is said about the parts of the light that are not reflected by things that we see?

CHAPTER XXVIII.
MORE ABOUT COLOR.

YOU SEE that the color of a thing is not a part of the thing itself. It is something which the thing throws off or lets pass through it. The color of a thing depends upon what a thing will do to the light when the light comes to it. It has no color in the dark. Its color is made out of the light that shines on it.

Color is something that is made every moment. The color that you see now in any thing is made now, out of the light that is shining. If a piece of cloth looks blue to you, it makes the blue color out of the light while you are looking at it. The dyer did not really make the color. The dye that he put it into altered the cloth so that it would make a blue color go to your eye from the light that comes to the cloth.

You have seen changeable silk. Here the colors change as the silk is moved. The reason is that, as the light strikes it in different ways, different parts of the light are reflected from it, and come to our eyes. For the same reason, as the hanging prisms of a chandelier or a girandole move, you see the colors in them change. So when the wind moves the tree covered with ice, or blows along the little pieces scattered on the ground, you see the same play of colors.

There is another fact which shows that color is not a fixed thing. It changes with different kinds of light. The light of a lamp or of a fire is not exactly like the light of the sun. It is not so white, and so we very often find that a thing which we have looked at in the evening has quite a different color when we come to see it by the sunlight. A piece of cloth that looks white by candlelight may look quite yellow the next morning by the light of day.

I have told you in Part First about the great variety of colors in flowers. All these colors are made out of the same light. If a flower is yellow, it is because the yellow part of the light is sent to our eyes, while the flower, as we may say, keeps the other six colors to itself. Some flowers are more yellow than others. The reason is that they reflect more of the yellow part of the light. Some leaves are greener than others because they send to our eyes more of the green part of the light.

In some flowers there are different colors close by each other. In the iris you have the blue and the yellow. Here one part of the flower sends to your eye the blue part of the light, and another the yellow part. In some flowers you see white close by other colors. Thus one kind of poppy is white except by the edges, which look as if they had been dipped in a red dye. How singular it is that, while some parts of the flower are fitted to send to your eye one color alone, the other parts send all the seven colors mixed together so as to make a white color!

Look, too, at the gradation of colors. This is very beautiful in some flowers. In some roses you see the red color shade off into white. You look at one of its leaves, and see a part of it that is quite red, and as your eye goes from this part, the red is less and less deep, till at the very edge it is all gone. Now remember that the more of the red part of the light is reflected, and the less there is of the other parts, the greater is the redness, and see how wonderful all this is. How nicely must the flower be made in order to give this shading off! In the very red part a great deal of the red color is sent to our eyes, and none of the other colors. Then from the part close by it a little less of the red is sent, and a little of the other colors mixed together is also sent; and so on, a little less and a little less of the red, and a little more and a little more of the others, till at the edge all the colors are reflected so as to make it look white.

In Part First I told you that the colors of flowers are made out of the sap, and now in this chapter I have told you that the colors are really made from the light. It may seem to you that both of these things can not be true; but while the colors are made from the light, in one sense they may also be said to be made from the sap. The flowers are so made out of the sap that they reflect the right colors from the light that comes to them. Thus a blue flower is so made as to reflect the blue part of the light. It is just as blue cloth is fitted by the dye that it is put into to reflect blue; and as we say that the dyer makes the cloth blue by his dye, so we say that the flower is made blue from the sap.

I have told you in Part First about the change of color in the leaves in the autumn. All the summer the leaves send the green part of the light to your eyes; but when autumn comes there is some change made in them, so that some kinds of leaves reflect the red part of the light, some the yellow, some the orange, etc.

I have told you about the great variety of colors in the plumage of birds and in the coverings of insects. This variety is all owing to the different ways in which the light is reflected. Some reflect one of the seven colors of the light, and others some other color. Some that reflect all the colors of the light are white, as the swan; and some that reflect none of them look black, as the crow.

Some of the most splendid displays of colors that can be

witnessed we occasionally see in the clouds at morning or evening. Now all this is caused by nothing but sunlight and water, for you know that the clouds are made up of water in the shape of fog. The light, as we may say, paints these gorgeous colors upon the drops of water as they hang in the air. The reason that we see these displays of colors in the clouds only at morning and evening is, that the light from the sun strikes them in the right way then. It strikes them in such a way that some of the colors are reflected to our eyes, while others are not. The most common color reflected to our eyes by the clouds is red.

You can see in other things that the color of a thing depends on the way in which the light strikes it, and is reflected to your eyes. You see this in the changeable silk. As you move it, the light strikes it differently, and so different colors are reflected to your eyes. When you see the ice scattered on the ground from the trees in winter, shining in the bright sun, you see in one direction all the colors of the rainbow sparkling from the millions of pieces of ice; but if you look in the opposite direction you see none of these colors, but the ice looks white. Why is this? It is because the light on one side of you strikes the ice and is reflected differently from what it is on the other side. And you know that it is not after every thunder-shower that you see a rainbow. The light must strike the rain, and be reflected to your eyes in a particular way, in order to let you see the light divided up in the rain into its seven colors in the bow. You never see a rainbow if the rain is in the same direction with the sun. If the sun is in the west, the rain must be in the east to have the bow form; so that you are between the sun and the rain, with your back to the sun, as you see the bow. Sometimes a rainbow is seen in the morning, when a cloud comes from the east and it clears off by the cloud's passing to the west. But this seldom happens, and the rainbow is commonly seen in the latter part of the day, the cloud coming from the west and passing off to the east.

Questions.—*What* is the color of a thing? Does the dyer make color? What does he do? What is said about changeable silk? Mention some other things in which we see the colors change. What is said about the changes of color in different kinds of light? How are the different colors of flowers made? How is it when there are different colors in the same flower? What is said about the shading off of colors? In what sense are the colors of flowers made from the light? And in what sense are they made from the sap? What is said about the change of color in leaves in autumn? What is said about the colors of birds and insects? Tell about the colors of the clouds. Why do we see them at morning and evening? What is said about the way in which light strikes a thing and is reflected to our eyes? Where and in what part of the day do you commonly see the rainbow? Explain this.

CHAPTER XXIX.
ELECTRICITY.

WHEN YOU see the lightning in a thunder-storm, you would think it strange if I should tell you that there is lightning in every thing; but so it is, as you will see. Did you ever have your fingers tingle, and hear a snapping when you stroked a cat's back? This is because you waked up, as we may say, the lightning in her fur and in your hand together. There is lightning in you as well as in the cat. It only needs a little rubbing to show it. I have known persons to light the gas with the lightning that is in them as readily as you would with a match. They wake up or excite the lightning by walking across the carpet, rubbing their feet on it as they go, and then put a finger to the open gas-burner. A spark of lightning goes to it from the finger and lights the gas.

It is in very clear cold weather that it is most easy to excite the lightning or electricity that is in different things. It is then that you can make the cat's fur snap. Then, too, silk things will snap when you rub them or fold them up.

Though it is really lightning that is made by rubbing things, we do not call it so. We call it electricity. We did not know that lightning and electricity were the same thing till Dr. Franklin showed that they were. He found it out by an experiment with a kite, which I will relate to you after I have told you some other things about electricity.

You can make electricity more easily by rubbing some things than by rubbing others. I have already told you how easily it is waked up on the cat's back by stroking it. If you rub a stick of sealing-wax back and forth rapidly across your coat sleeve, you wake up a good deal of electricity for so small a thing. It is shown in this way: If you bring the sealing-wax near some light thing like down, this will cling to it for a moment, and then fly off again, as if it did not like the sealing-wax. It is the electricity which you have excited that does this.

A good deal of electricity can be made by rubbing glass.

In the machine which is used in making electricity for experiments there is a large glass cylinder, which is turned round quickly against a leather rubber that has a preparation of mercury on it.

In this machine, represented here, *a* is the glass cylinder, and *b b* are the wheels by which it is made to turn round. These wheels are worked by the handle which you see on the lower one. The rubber is pressed against the glass cylinder on the side of it that you do not see. You can see the standard that holds the rubber. At *c* is a piece of oiled silk that is fastened to the rubber, and lies upon the glass cylinder, serving to keep it free from dust. At *d* you see a receiver, as it is called, which receives the electricity as fast as it is produced. This is made of brass, and has a glass standard, *e*. Now, as the machine is worked, the electricity excited by the rubber and the glass passes off continually to this receiver, and there it stays collected on the surface of it, for it can not go down the standard. Why is this? you will ask. It is because glass, though a very good thing to make electricity with, is very slow to let the electricity pass over it. I shall tell you more about this soon.

Well, there is the electricity all over this receiver. It stays there because it can not get away. It is ready to go whenever it can get a chance. You would find this out if you should put your finger near that knob that you see on the end of the receiver. Almost all of the electricity in the receiver would pass through your finger into your body, and give you a shock; and if there was much electricity in the receiver, the shock would be harder than you would wish to bear.

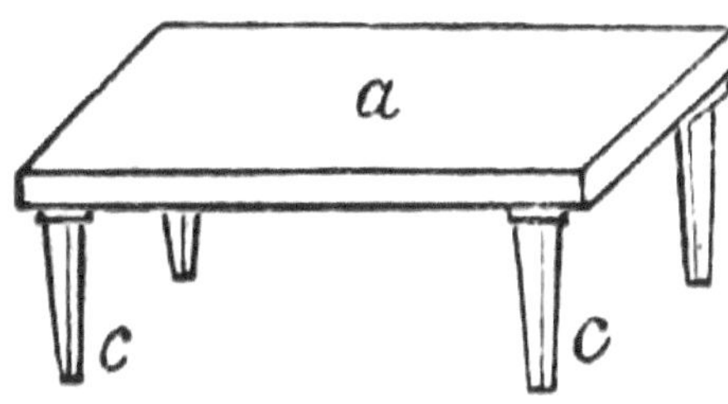

Now a person can act as a receiver and be charged with electricity just as this brass receiver is. It can be done in this way. The person stands on a stool, such as you see here. The top of this, *a*, is wood, and the legs, *c*, *c*, are glass. These glass legs answer for him as the glass standard does for the receiver of the machine. They prevent the electricity that he gets from passing off. If he stood on the floor, it would pass to the floor as fast as it came to him. As he stands on this stool, he holds in his hand a chain that is fastened to the knob on the end of the brass receiver. You can see now what will happen when the machine is worked. The electricity that goes from the glass cylinder to the receiver does not all stay there, but most of it goes on through the chain to the person on the stool. It can not get from him to the floor, for the glass legs prevent this. Therefore, after working the machine some time, he becomes filled with electricity, just as the brass receiver does on its glass standard, and you can receive a shock from him, for he is now a receiver. If you put your finger to his nose, or chin, or any other part, the electricity will pass to you with a spark, and will give you a shock.

How electricity affects the hair.

A curious effect is produced on the hair when one is thus charged with electricity. The hair stands out straight. This effect is seen in a very amusing way by having a figure of a head with hair on it fastened to the receiver. The hair will stand out as you see here.

The electricity that is collected on the brass receiver can be taken off and be bottled up, as we may say, so as to be convenient for use. This can be done with what is called the Leyden jar, as represented here. This is a glass jar coated inside and out with tin foil to within a few inches of the top. Then there is a knob on the end of a wire that extends down into the jar. Now see how we do this bottling up of the electricity. The knob of the jar

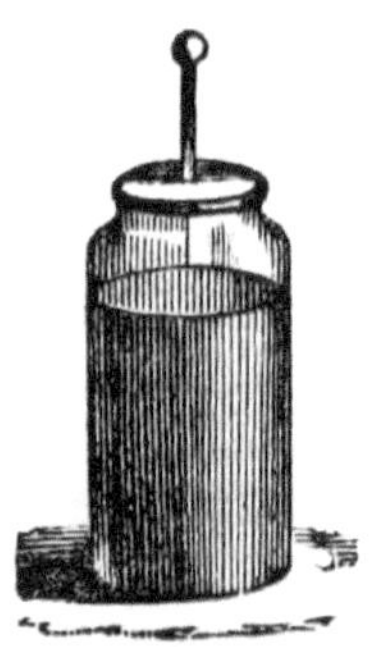

Bottling it up in the Leyden jar.

is held close to the knob of the receiver as the machine is worked. The electricity, therefore, passes to the knob of the jar, and by the wire to all the inside of the jar where the tin foil is. It can not get outside, because it can not pass over or through the glass.

So, then, the electricity is shut up in the jar, but it is ready to come out when it has a way made for it to come. If the inside foil and the outside foil be connected together by something that will let the electricity pass through it, it will come out of the jar. You can be that something if you please. If you put one hand on the tin foil on the outside, and touch the other to the knob on the end of the wire, the electricity will come out by the wire, and give you a shock in your wrists, and elbows, and chest.

A great many persons can take a shock in this way at the same time. Suppose there are a hundred persons standing in a ring and taking hold of each other's hands. Let there be two in this ring that do not have hold of each other. Now, if one of these touches the jar on the outside, and the other touches the knob, the whole hundred will feel a shock at the same time, for the electricity will go through them all around the whole ring as quick as lightning, as we say; and it is, in this case, really so, for the electricity is lightning. And so, when in the telegraph the electricity passes along the wire, it takes almost no time for it to go very great distances.

Sometimes a great deal of electricity is collected in a number of these jars, which are connected together in such a way that the electricity can be discharged from them all at once. A collection of jars thus connected, as represented here, is called an electrical battery. There is need of

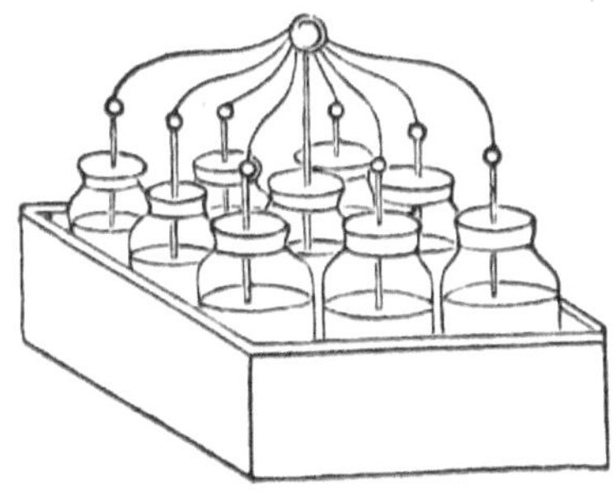

great care in experimenting with a battery; for if, when the jars are well filled, they should all be discharged into any one, he would be killed in the same way that one is who is struck with lightning.

You remember that I told you, in Part Second, Chapter XXV., that there are some animals that have electrical machines or batteries in them. There are only a few such animals, and they are great curiosities. They can fire off their batteries when they please, but exactly how they do it we do not know. These batteries are more nicely and curiously made than any that man makes, and have much more power. They are so small that it is wonderful that they can give such severe shocks.

Questions.—Why does the fur of a cat sometimes snap when it is stroked? How can some persons light the gas by their electricity? When is the best time to wake up electricity? Who discovered that lightning and electricity were the same thing? What things will give out electricity easily when rubbed? Describe the electrical machine. Why does the electricity stay on the receiver? What will happen if you put your finger near the knob on the end of it? Tell how a person can be made to act as a receiver. Why can not the electricity go from him into the floor? Tell about taking shocks from him. What effect is produced on his hair? Tell how electricity can be bottled up. How can you get it out of the bottle again? Tell how a great many persons can take a shock from the jar at the same time. What is said about the quickness with which electricity goes? What is an electrical battery? What is said about electricity in some animals?

CHAPTER XXX.

MORE ABOUT ELECTRICITY.

ELECTRICITY PASSES through some things more easily than it does through others. Those that it passes through easily are said to be good conductors of electricity. There are some things that let so very little pass through or over them that they are called non-conductors. Such are glass and silk. The different metals, copper, silver, iron, etc., are good conductors.

You have seen how a lightning-rod is fastened to a house. It rests against pieces of wood. Observe what the object of this is. Iron lets the electricity or lightning pass much more easily than the wood does. Now, if the rod was fastened to the house by iron supports, the lightning, as it came down the rod, might go into the house by some of these supports, instead of going down by the rod into the ground.

The iron is called a good conductor, while the wood is a poor conductor. Glass is a poorer conductor still. It is so poor a conductor that it is called a non-conductor, as I have before told you. It is for this reason that the telegraph wires are fastened to glass knobs on the posts. The object is to have all the electricity go along on the wires, and not let any of it escape down the posts. If a very little of it should escape down each post, by the time it came to the end of the journey there might not be enough left to do any good.

Silk, I have told you, is one of the non-conductors. Dr. Franklin made use of silk in the experiment by which he discovered that lightning and electricity are the same thing.

DR. FRANKLIN EXPERIMENTING WITH HIS KITE.

He managed in this way: He made his kite of a large silk handkerchief instead of paper. He had on it a pointed iron wire, and the string of the kite was fastened to this wire. This kite he sent up in a thunder-storm, when there was a plenty of electricity in the clouds. The iron wire would of course receive some of the electricity, and it would not go from the wire to the kite, because that was made of silk, which, you know, is a non-conductor. It would go down the string, this being tied to the wire. Passing down the string, it would go to Dr. Franklin's hand, and down his body into the earth. It would do this silently, because it would keep going a little at a time all the while. But he managed to prevent the electricity from coming to his hand. He stopped it on the way. He did this by tying a silk ribbon to the hemp string, and holding the kite by this ribbon, as you see in the picture. The electricity could not go through this silk, and so it staid in the hemp string.

Dr. Franklin now fastened a key to the end of the hemp string. A great deal of the electricity now passed to the key, because the metal of which the key was made was so good a conductor. It was a much better conductor than the string, and so the electricity, as we may say, spread all over it. It was a real receiver of the electricity, like the brass receiver of the electrical machine. Accordingly, when Franklin put his knuckle near the key, he received a shock from it, just as one does from the knob of the brass receiver. After a little time it began to rain, and then the shocks were harder. The reason was, that the string, when wet, was a better conductor than when dry, and so the electricity came on it faster to the key.

In this way Dr. Franklin drew the lightning down from the clouds in so small a quantity that he could find out what it was. He found that it was just the same as the electricity that we make by the electrical machine, and he could bottle it up in the same way that we do the electricity from the brass receiver. This he could do by holding the Leyden jar with its brass knob to the key. The electricity would go into it just as it does from the receiver when we are working the machine.

Before Franklin tried this experiment with his kite it was supposed that the lightning was electricity, but it was only supposition. No one knew that it was so. It was never proved till Franklin sent up his silk kite to find out about it. It was supposed that lightning was electricity simply because the effects of lightning were similar to the effects of the electricity of the machine when a great deal of this electricity was made. Experiments were tried which showed that the machine electricity, when there was enough of it, tore things to pieces, and killed animals, just as lightning does; but the difficulty was that no one had ever seen what a little of the lightning would do. This Franklin found out by bringing some of it down out of the clouds by the string of his kite, and bottling it up for use in the Leyden jar. Before his experiments nothing was known about lightning except as it was seen in large quantities going from cloud to cloud, or coming down to the earth and shivering a tree, or plowing up the ground, or perhaps killing some animal or some man. Nothing was known of it in a small way until Franklin showed us so much about it by his experiments.

It was these experiments of Dr. Franklin that suggested the use of lightning-rods. These rods protect houses in two ways. One way is this: If the lightning comes down directly toward a house in a considerable quantity, instead of striking the house, it will go down the rod into the ground. Another way in which the rod affords protection is this: Sometimes the lightning or electricity goes down the rod from the clouds above in a continual stream of very small quantity, just as it went down the string of Franklin's kite. A cloud with a great deal of electricity in it often has it discharged in this quiet way.

You know that there are points on the ends of lightning-rods. These are to receive the electricity. It will go to them better than it would to a blunt rod. We know that this is so in working the electrical machine described on page 145. Instead of having simply the blunt end of the receiver near the rubber, there are points on that end of it to receive the electricity as fast as it is made.

Questions.—*What* things are called good conductors of electricity? What are called non-conductors? Why are lightning-rods supported against a building by pieces of wood? Why are telegraph wires fastened to glass knobs on the posts? How did Franklin make his kite? Why did he make it of silk instead of paper? How did he prevent the electricity that came down the string from going through him into the ground? Why was the key so good a receiver of electricity? Tell about his taking shocks from it. Why were the shocks stronger after it began to rain? How did he bottle up the electricity that he thus drew from the clouds? Why was it supposed before his experiment that electricity and lightning were the same thing? Why was it not known to be so? In what two ways do lightning-rods protect houses? Why are lightning-rods pointed?

CHAPTER XXXI.

MAGNETISM.

IN SOME parts of the world a kind of iron ore is found which is called loadstone. It has a peculiar power. It attracts iron very strongly. Hold it close to some iron filings, and they will cling to it in quite a cluster as you raise it up; so, also, you can take up with it a great many needles, and if it be a large piece of the ore, it will hold up a very heavy weight. This power which the loadstone has we call magnetism.

Now this power in the loadstone can be communicated to iron and steel. If a loadstone be moved along in a particular way on a piece of iron or steel several times, the iron or steel will receive this power, and will act as a magnet, just as the loadstone does. Common iron will not keep the power long, but steel will.

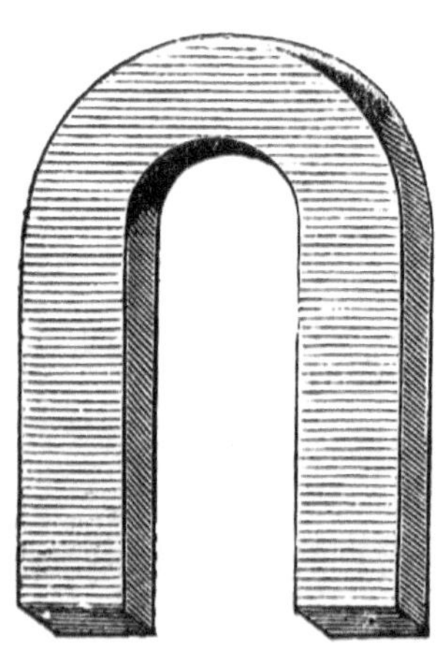

How common magnets are made.

Most of the magnets that we see are not real loadstone, but they are steel that has been magnetized by the loadstone. They are commonly made in a horse-shoe shape, as represented here. They will hold up a considerable weight of iron, and sometimes twenty-eight times their own weight; and it is curious that a magnet which holds a weight all the time will have its power increased. There is no tiring out of its power; and, on the contrary, if you give a magnet nothing to do, its power will grow weak—it will not be able to hold up so much weight as it did at first. It is for this reason that magnets are never left without a weight hanging to them.

You have perhaps often been amused in making toy fishes or ducks swim about in the water with a little magnet. You have seen how readily they follow the magnet, and how quickly they spring forward to hold on to it, if you happen to put it very near them. This is because each has a little piece of steel in its mouth which is attracted by the magnet.

How very strange this power of the magnet is! It is not any thing that you can see, and yet there the power is. You see what it does. This unseen power in the magnet takes hold of things and draws them to it, as our hand, that we see, takes hold of things and draws them to us. How it does this we do not understand.

This power does not seem to do much at any distance from the magnet. If you hold your little magnet quite away from the toy duck or fish, it will not make it move; but bring it near, and now you see it follows the magnet all about; and if you bring it very near, the little thing, as quick as a wink, darts forward and clings to the magnet very firmly. So, too, if you bring an iron weight slowly nearer and nearer to a large magnet, there does not seem to be any influence from the magnet upon it till you bring it very near, and then all at once away goes the weight out of your hand to cling to the magnet. It is as if the magnet had very short hands that could not reach far; but so far as they do reach, they are very strong and hold fast. Whenever you get a chance to see a magnet of considerable size, you can try this experiment.

You have heard of the mariner's compass, but perhaps it has never been explained to you. There is a slender piece of steel in this compass which always points to the north. It is balanced on a pivot, so that it can move around easily to the one side or the other. However much it is jostled, however much you may turn the box of the compass round, this needle is always tremblingly but surely pointing one way. This needle is a magnetized piece of steel. We may consider the whole earth, with all its loadstone and iron, as a great magnet, and it is the influence of the earth upon the magnetic needle that makes it always point to the north. You can at any time make a mariner's compass in a very simple way. All that you need is a magnetized needle, a piece of cork, and a bowl of water. Put the cork in the water, and lay the needle across it, and the needle will point north and south. You see how this is. The cork moves so readily in the water that the needle in getting right can turn it as is needed. It will turn almost as easily as the needle does on its pivot in the compasses that are made.

The mariner's compass, you can see, must be of great use to the mariner. When he is far out at sea, where no land can be seen, he always knows by this which way north is, and so he judges how to direct his vessel in order to reach the desired port. If it were always sunshine, he would do very well without the compass, for he could tell by the sun which way was north, and south, and east, and west; but in stormy weather and in the night he would be at a loss. At such times, by looking at his ever faithful compass, he knows in what direction to steer his vessel. You remember about the voyage and shipwreck of the apostle Paul, related in the 27th chapter of Acts. Nothing was known about the mariner's compass then. So "when neither sun nor stars in many days appeared," they did not know all this time where the wind was carrying them. Perhaps if they had had a compass on board they could have kept the ship from going ashore and being dashed to pieces.

Magnetism often has a great deal to do with electricity, and some persons suppose them to be the same thing. Electricity may wake up the magnetic power to even a wonderful degree. In Morse's telegraph there are both electrical machinery and magnetic machinery. The electricity that comes over the wires excites the magnetic machinery, and it is this magnetism that delivers the message sent by the electricity. Just how this operates you can understand better when you are a little older.

Questions.—*What* is loadstone? What peculiar power has it? To what can it communicate this power? What are the magnets in common use? Why is a weight always kept hanging to a magnet? Tell about the toy fishes and ducks. What is said about the strangeness of the magnetic power? Does it do much at any distance from the magnet? Give the illustrations. What is the mariner's compass? How can you make one? What makes the needle always point to the north? How is the mariner's compass of use at sea? Tell about St. Paul's shipwreck. What effect does electricity often produce upon magnetism? How is it in Morse's telegraph?

CHAPTER XXXII.

GRAVITATION.

I F I should ask you why things in the air fall to the ground, you would probably say it is because it is downward, and every thing must come down that is not held up in some way. But what is down, and what is up? This I will explain to you.

The earth, as perhaps you know, is as round as an orange, and people can travel around it just as you can pass your finger around over the orange. This, indeed, was one of the ways in which it was found to be round. Another proof of its being round is this: As you see a ship go out to sea, if you watch it for a long time, after a while the body of the ship will go out of sight, and you will see nothing but the sails, and then the sails will gradually go out of sight also. What does this prove? Why, that the water is not flat, as it appears to be to us, but that it makes a part of the rounded surface of the earth. This figure will make this plain to you.

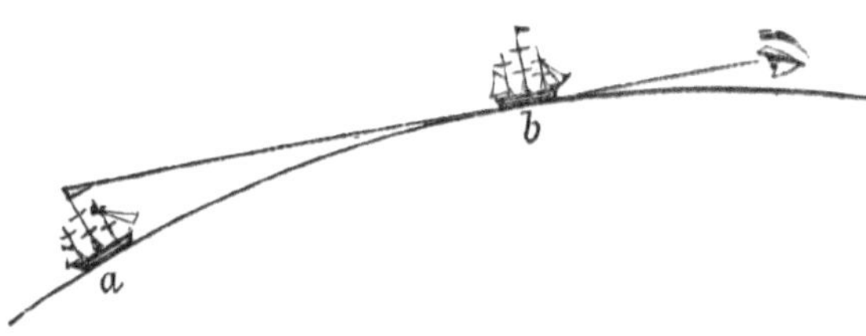

The eye that is represented sees the whole ship at *b*; but when it gets as far as *a*, the eye can see only the streamer at the top of the mast.

The reason that we do not see that the earth is round is that we are so small and the earth is so large. We see that a globe is round, but it probably seems flat to any little fly that lights upon it, just as the earth does to us.

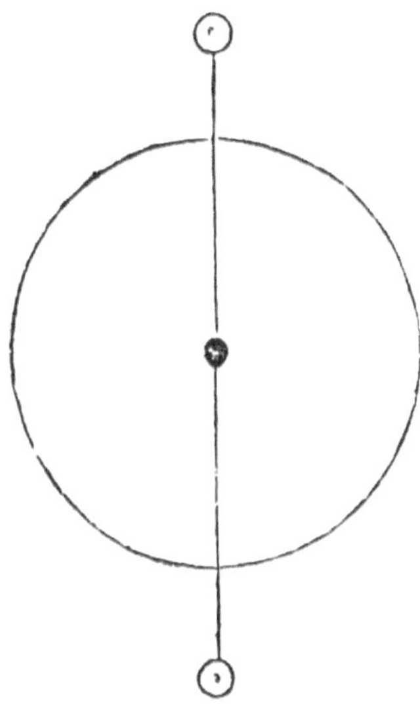

You can see, then, that as the earth is round, what is down to people on the other side of the earth is up to us. If a boy there throw up a ball at the same time that you throw up one here, the two balls fall toward each other when they come to the ground.

What we call down, then, is simply toward the ground, or, rather, it is toward the middle of the earth, for we say down in a well or down in the ground. Indeed, if any thing could keep on in the same line in which it falls, it would go right to the centre of the earth. If the ball which you throw up and the ball thrown up by a boy on the other side of the earth should keep on in the ground in the same direction that they fall, they would meet exactly at the earth's centre. This is represented in this figure. The circle represents the round earth. The lines drawn from the two falling balls to the middle of the circle show how they would come together at the centre of the earth if they could keep on, instead of being stopped when they reach the ground. And all the things that are falling any where on the earth are going toward the same point.

Now why is this? What is it that makes things in the air come to the ground when they are not held up? They do not come down of themselves. They are drawn down. The earth attracts or draws them. How it does this we do not know. We can not see how it is done, but the earth does it as really as if we could see it put up a hand and pull things down.

There are other kinds of attraction that operate in a way that we can not see nor understand. There is the attraction of magnetism. If, as I have told you in the last chapter, you bring a magnet toward a piece of iron or steel, for example a needle, when you get it quite near, all at once the needle will go to the magnet and stick to it. You can not see any thing between the magnet and the needle to draw the needle to it. You only know that the needle is drawn or attracted, but you do not know how this is done.

It is just so with this attraction which the earth has for all things, drawing them to it. You can not see any thing any more than you can in the case of the magnet and the needle, but the attraction is as real as if you could see it. You can see what it does, as you can see what is done by the attraction of magnetism.

This attraction is called the attraction of gravitation. It is stronger with some things than it is with others. When any thing is drawn strongly to the earth, we say that it is very heavy; but when a thing is not strongly attracted, we say that it is light. When you take hold of a stone to raise it up, you have this attraction of the earth acting against you. This is pulling the stone down while your muscles are trying to raise it. If the stone is very large, the earth attracts it so strongly that the force of your muscles can not overcome the attraction. If the earth would only stop pulling upon the stone, you could raise it easily enough.

You see, then, what weight is. It is the pressure made by a thing as the earth draws or attracts it to itself. The stronger this attraction is, the greater is the pressure—that is, the weight. If you lay a foot-ball upon your foot, you scarcely feel the pressure of it; but if you lay a stone of the same size upon your foot, it presses very hard. The reason is, that the stone is drawn toward the earth much more strongly than the foot-ball. The foot-ball is drawn lightly, and so presses a little; but the stone is drawn much, and so presses a great deal. Your foot, being between the stone and the earth, is pressed by the stone as the earth draws it to itself. It is just as you would be pressed if you were between me and some one that I was drawing toward me.

The reason that the stone is attracted more strongly, or has more weight, than the foot-ball is, that there is more substance to it—that is, the particles in it are closer together. So lead or iron is heavier than wood, because the wood is much more porous: you can see pores and spaces in it, while you can not in the lead and iron. You remember what I told you about the hot-air balloon. This has not as much weight as it would have if it were full of cold air. The reason is, that the particles of cold air are closer together than the particles of hot air; for, you know, heat swells air—that is, it puts its particles farther apart.

If you drop a bag of feathers, it falls to the ground because the earth attracts it. If, now, you drop a stone upon this bag, it sinks down in the midst of it, because the earth attracts it much more strongly than it does the loose feathers. It is for the same reason that a stone sinks in water. The earth attracts the stone more than it does the water.

Wood will not sink in water as the stone does, for it is not drawn down to the earth as hard as the water is; but wood will fall through air to the ground, because the wood is attracted by the earth more strongly than the air is. If you put a block of wood down in the water, and then let it go, it rises to the surface. Why is this? It is because the water, being more strongly drawn down by the earth than the wood, pushes the wood up out of the way. It is for the same reason that the balloon filled with hot air or with light gas rises. It is not attracted to the earth as much as the cool air around it is, and so it is pushed up out of the way.

Every thing, you see, then, is attracted by the earth. The air itself is kept close to the earth by this attraction. It makes a sea, as we may say, all around the earth about forty-five miles deep. Beyond that there is no air except around some of the other worlds that we see far off in the sky. Now the air would fly off and spread every where among the stars if the earth did not attract it and thus keep it around itself. The air moves about freely like the water, but it can not fly away from the earth any more than the water can. The earth keeps both its air and water all to itself by attraction.

Every thing gets as close to the earth as it can, because every thing is attracted by the earth. There is nothing that is of itself disposed to go up, but every thing, even the air, is pressing down, the heaviest always getting the lowest if it can, and there is sometimes a sort of strife as to which shall be lowest. When a stone is put upon a heap of feathers, the earth pulls upon it so much harder than it does on the feathers that the stone presses to get through them to the earth; but as it can not thrust them out of the way, it crushes them down in the struggle to get below them. The struggle is a different one with the stone in water. The water clings to the earth, but it is easily pushed away by the stone as it tries to get below the water. Even in the going up of a balloon you can see the same struggle. It would stay down if it could. It goes up, as I have before told you, simply because the cold air about it, being more strongly attracted by the earth than the balloon is, tries to get below the balloon. If the cold air could be taken away, the balloon would stay down, for the same reason that a block of wood would remain in the bottom of a bowl if there were no water in it. The block, attracted by the earth, will stay as near the earth as it can. The water pushes it up because it is attracted by the earth more than the block is, and for the same reason the air pushes up the balloon.

Questions.—*What* is the common idea about the falling of things to the ground? What is one of the proofs that the earth is round? What is another proof? Why can not we see that the earth is round? What is meant by down and up? Tell what is represented by the figure. What is it that makes things fall to the ground? Give the comparison about the attraction of magnetism. What is said about the earth's attracting some things more strongly than others? What is weight? Explain by telling about the foot-ball and the stone. Why is the stone attracted more strongly than the foot-ball? Why are lead and iron heavier than wood? Why is a hot-air balloon lighter than the air around it? Tell about the feathers and the stone. Why will not wood sink in water as stone does? Give the comparison between the block of wood and the balloon. What is said about the earth's attracting the air? Is there any thing that does not press down? Which always gets the lowest if it can? Tell about the stone put on the feathers and dropped in the water. Give the comparison between the balloon and the block of wood in a bowl.

CHAPTER XXXIII.

THE MOTION OF THE EARTH.

WHEN A boy throws a ball up into the air, he thinks that it comes down of itself. He thinks that it comes down merely because the force with which he sent it up is spent or lost; but this is not so. It is pulled down. The earth pulls it down. The earth is pulling upon it all the time as it goes up, and gradually overcomes the force with which he threw it up.

There is another thing that helps to overcome the force by which the ball is sent up. It is the resistance of the air. As the ball goes up, it has to spend a part of its force in pushing the air away to make a path for itself.

These two things—the pulling of the earth and the resistance of the air—gradually stop the going up of the ball. If there was no air, and if the earth would let the ball go, instead of drawing upon it, it would not come down. It would fly off out of sight; and more than that, it would never stop till something stopped it. It could never stop of itself.

This, perhaps, seems strange to you; but look at it. A ball, you know, has no power. It lies still if you do not touch it. It can not move itself, and, for the same reason, it can not stop itself. Once set it agoing, and it would move on forever if it was not stopped by something.

This is true of all matter that is not alive. You can set yourself in motion, and stop yourself, for you are alive; but common dead matter can do neither. It moves because it is moved, and it stops because it is stopped by something.

Now the earth is a ball that is always moving. It never stops for an instant, but is all the time rolling on around and around the sun. God a long time ago set it agoing, and it never has been still since. It takes a year for it to go round the sun; and how fast do you think it goes? About 68,000 miles an hour—that is, over a thousand miles every minute. This is two thousand times as fast as the cars go when they are going very fast indeed. What a ride we are taking on this round ball of earth!

But you will ask why it is that we do not feel any thing of this motion, or know something about it, just as we do about the motion of traveling. The reason of this is very easily seen. Just observe how it is that you know about the motion in traveling. You see trees, houses, fences, etc., as you pass by them. You feel the air as you go through it. If the motion is uneven, you feel it. It is by these things that you know that you are moving along. But as we are carried along on the earth as it goes around the sun, there are none of these things to let us know that we are moving. Every thing goes along with us—trees, houses, fences, and every thing else. We do not go through the air, but the air goes along with us. Then, too, the motion is very even. The earth is not jostled and jarred in its course.

Sometimes, when you are riding in the cars, you hardly seem to move at all, though you may be really going very fast. The reason of this is plain. First, the motion is very even; then the air that is in the car goes along with you, though the air that is outside does not; and the people in the car that you are looking at are going along with you also.

But the moment you look out of the car window you know that the cars are going quite rapidly, because you see that you are going so fast by the trees and houses. So, too, if the cars come to a place where the rails are not so even, the irregular motion lets you know that you are going fast. Sometimes, when you seem to be going along quite moderately, because the rails are so even and the road is so straight, all at once you seem to be twitched along with a very sudden, quick start. It seems to you as if the cars suddenly went a great deal faster, but it is not so. The cars are really moving no faster than before. A turn in the road makes it seem so, because it makes the motion irregular instead of even.

Now, if the motion of the cars were perfectly even, and you did not look out, you would not know that they were moving at all. Just so it is with the earth. Its motion is so even that we do not feel that it moves at all, though it is carrying us two thousand times as fast as the cars carry us when they are going thirty-four miles in an hour.

It is true that we look away from the earth as we are riding along on it just as we look out of the cars; but the sun, and moon, and stars that we see are so far off that we can not tell by looking at them that the earth is moving. It seems to us to be standing still. For the same reason, the cars do not seem to be moving if you look at things a great way off, instead of those that are near by.

A great many mistakes have been made about the motion of the earth, for things are not always as they appear to be. It seems to us as if the earth did not move at all; while the sun, and moon, and stars seem to move, because they are not always in the same direction from us. We look one way for them at one time, and another way at another time. Now they do move, but not in the way that they appear to us. The sun seems to rise, and go up and up, and then go down in the west. But this is not so. This is all owing to a motion of the earth that I have not yet told you about. As the earth goes round the sun, it also turns every day around on itself. It is this motion that makes day and night for us. As the earth thus rolls over, where the sun shines upon it it is day, and where it does not shine upon it it is night.

The earth, then, has two motions. First, it goes round the sun. This, as I have told you, takes a year; but in every twenty-four hours it turns over also. This is its second motion. It performs this 365 times while it is doing the first motion once.

These two motions can be made plain to you with a candle and some round thing, as an orange. Let the candle represent the sun. Carry the orange around it in a circle, and this will represent the earth going round the sun. Now, by turning the orange so that the candle will shine upon one part of it, and then upon another, and so on all around it, you will see how the second motion of the earth is done, and how night and day are made. Any thing that you do not quite understand about this your teacher will explain to you.

The earth, I have told you, turns around on itself 365 times in a year. But there is one thing about this that I must mention to you. It takes about six hours over the 365 days for the earth to go round the sun. Now what is done with this six hours in reckoning the year? It is managed in this way. It is a quarter part of twenty-four hours, or a day, and so, to make the reckoning come right, a day is added every fourth year. It is added to the month of February. Every fourth year this month has twenty-nine days instead of twenty-eight, and the year is called leap year.

Astronomers have discovered a great many things about

the shape and the motions of the earth. Before these were understood, people supposed that the earth was still, and was flat instead of round, and that the sun really rose in the east and set in the west; and it seems so to every body now that has not learned what the astronomers have discovered. A bright little boy said to a lady who was teaching him about the earth, You don't mean to say that the world is round? I know that it isn't. I can see that it is flat with my own eyes. She assured him that the earth was round, but he could not believe it, and replied, Well, I shall ask my father, for gentlemen commonly know more about such things than ladies do. You will think it strange when I tell you that, a little more than two hundred years ago, people generally believed as this little boy did, and that they put a learned man, named Galileo, into prison because he said that the earth was round, and that it went around the sun.

You will want to know something about the motion of the moon. As the earth goes round the sun, so the moon moves around the earth. It takes a little less than a month for it to get round the earth, and it goes around it about thirteen times a year. As I have told you in another chapter, the silvery light which the moon sheds upon us is the light of the sun reflected by the moon. Why it is that only a part of the moon shines upon us much of the time, I will explain to you. When there is a new moon, as it is termed, the moon is in such a position that we can see only a little of that part of it which the sun shines upon. But when the moon is at the full, it is in such a position that we see all of it that is lighted up by the sun. So when the moon quarters, as it is expressed, we see but a half of the lighted portion, and so on. All this is made plain by the opposite figure. S is the sun, E is the earth, and *a, b, c,* &c., the moon in dif-

ferent positions.
When the moon is
at *a* we can not see
any of it, because
it is between the
earth and the sun.
The sun shines
upon the half of
the moon that is

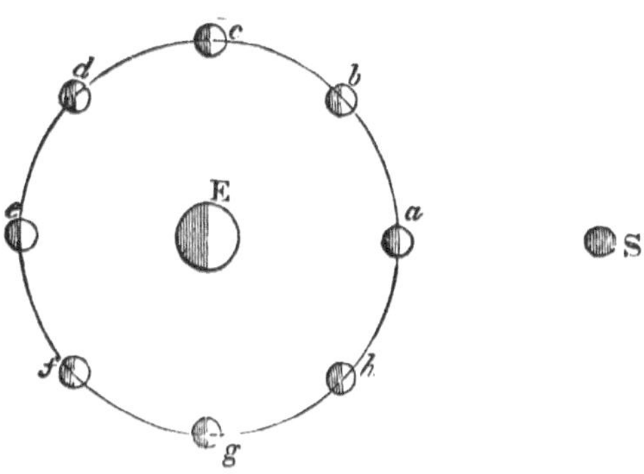

toward it, and this half is now all away from our sight. As
it leaves *a* we see a little of it, and a little more every night;
and when it gets to *b* we see a quarter of the part which the
sun shines upon. Then, when it comes to *c*, we see half of
it. When it is at *d* we see rather more than half: it is then
called gibbous. When it is at *e* we can see the whole of the
lighted-up part, and so the moon is full. Then at *f* it is gibbous again, and at *g* half moon.

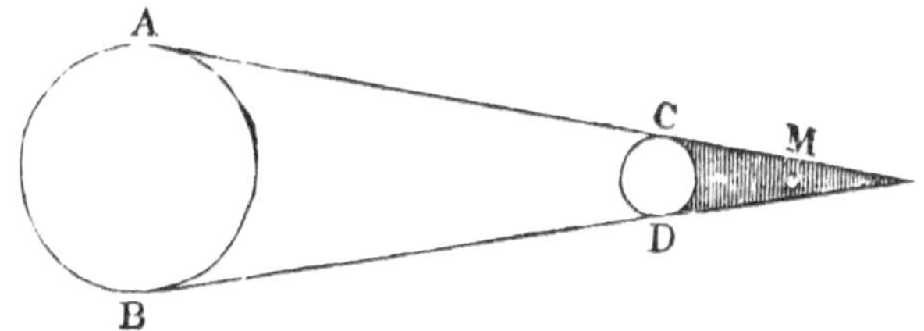

And now
you will want
to know how
an eclipse of
the moon
happens.
This I can
make plain to you by this figure. A B is the sun, C D the
earth, which is smaller than the sun, and M the moon,
which is much smaller than the earth. Now, as the sun
shines upon the earth, there is a dark shadow beyond the
earth, as represented. When the moon, therefore, happens
to pass through this shadow, it is in the dark, and no one
on the earth can see it till it comes out from the shadow.
While it is in the shadow there is an eclipse, as it is termed.

Questions.—What two things gradually stop the going up of a ball in the air? Could the ball stop of itself? Why can you set yourself going and stop yourself? How is it with dead matter? What is said about the earth? How fast does it move? How do you know about the motion in traveling? Why is it that sometimes, when the cars are going quite fast, you scarcely seem to be moving at all? How is it if you look out? How is it if the cars come to a place where the rails are uneven, or where there is a turn in the road? Give the comparison about looking out of the cars and looking away from the earth. Tell about the mistakes that have been made about the motion of the earth. How is it that day and night are made? Tell about the two motions of the earth. Describe how you would make these plain with a candle and an orange. Why is a day added to every fourth year, making it leap year? What did people suppose about the earth and sun before astronomers found out so much about them? Give the anecdote of the little boy. Tell about Galileo. Tell about the motion of the moon. Tell about the new moon and the full moon. Tell about the eclipse of the moon.

CHAPTER XXXIV.

FRICTION.

FRICTION SOMETIMES assists motion, and sometimes lessens or prevents it. I will tell you about this in this chapter.

When one is walking on ice, he finds that he must be careful, and he gets along slowly. The reason is that there is not enough rubbing or friction between his feet and the ice. When he walks on the ground, the friction between his feet and the ground keeps him from slipping, and he walks along with perfect ease. If sand or ashes be thrown upon the ice, the difficulty is removed, for this makes a friction that keeps him from slipping.

How swiftly the horse carries the sleigh along on the trodden snow! It is because there is so little friction on the smooth iron shoes of the runners; but let him come to a spot of bare ground, and he has to tug very hard to draw the sleigh along, because there is so much friction. You can not slide down hill on your sled when the ground is bare, simply because the friction is so great; but you can roll down on any thing that has wheels, because there is less friction with wheels than with runners.

In carrying heavy loads in carts down steep hills, there is a contrivance, which perhaps you have seen, to keep the carts from going down too fast. At the top of the hill the teamster stops his team, and fastens upon one of the wheels an iron shoe in such a way as to keep the wheel from turning round. The rubbing of this wheel with its shoe upon the ground makes the load go down slowly, and therefore safely.

It is the steam in the locomotive that makes it go. Did you ever think how it does this? It is by friction. This I will explain to you. You see the large wheels of the locomotive. These are called the driving-wheels, because it is the whirling round of these that makes the locomotive go. These wheels are whirled around by the steam machinery, as you can plainly see. It is different with the small wheels. They turn because the locomotive goes. It is just as the wheels of a carriage turn round when the horse draws it along. So the large wheels are to the locomotive what a horse is to a carriage, while the small wheels do as the common wheels of a carriage do.

Now see how it is that the driving-wheels carry along the locomotive. They do it by their rubbing on the rails of the road. If the rails and the wheels were very smooth indeed, the locomotive would not get along so well. We sometimes see this in a frosty morning, when the rails are very slippery. With the rails so smooth, the wheels slip; and they slip back as readily as forward, just as it is with any one walking on the ice. They sometimes throw some sand on the rails when they are icy to give the locomotive a start, as people scatter sand and ashes on icy sidewalks that they may walk easily on them.

After the wheels of a locomotive are once well started on the frosty rails, they will go well enough. Indeed, it is sometimes rather difficult to stop them, because they slide along so easily, for the motion is partly sliding and partly rolling when the rails are so smooth. It is for the same reason that one can not stop easily when he is running on the ice. If he is running on the ground, he can stop very readily, because the ground is rough, and his feet rub upon it, and they do not slip as they do on the ice.

The way that brakes, as they are called, stop a train of cars, I will explain to you. You know that the brakeman on each car turns around a ring-like thing as hard as he can when the signal is given to stop the cars. In doing this, he brings the brakes against the wheels of the cars, and the rubbing soon stops them.

When they want to stop the cars very quickly, they do another thing besides using the brakes. They manage to make the driving-wheels of the locomotive roll backward instead of forward. In this way the rubbing is backward on the rails; and as long as the locomotive is going forward, the wheels slide forward instead of rolling, as they commonly do.

You see that sometimes we want friction, and sometimes the less we have of it the better. We want the friction of the driving-wheels of a locomotive on the track. But in the middle of these wheels, where they turn round on their axles, we want to have as little friction as possible. It is for this reason that all the wheels of the cars and of the locomotive are kept oiled at this part. So, also, we grease the wheels of carriages and oil the joints of machinery to lessen the friction. You will recollect that in the chapter on the bones, in Part Second, I told you that the joints of our bodies are tipped with a very smooth substance, and that they are kept oiled, so that there may be little friction in their motions.

Friction is not confined to solid substances. Any substance can make friction. Water can do it. The rocks over which it flows, or against which it dashes, are worn by its constant friction, just as the constant friction of passing feet in the course of years wears the stone steps of a building which is much frequented.

Air, too, makes friction. It is by friction that the air, moving along over the smooth water, raises it into waves; and it is the friction of the air, as it passes over a field of grain, that gives it the wavy motion which makes it so beautiful.

Wherever there is motion on the earth, it is lessened more or less by friction. Nothing moves without rubbing something, but this is not so with the earth as it goes around the sun. As it flies through space so swiftly, it rubs against nothing, not even against air, for the air, as I have told you, goes along with it.

Questions.—*What* does friction do? What is said about walking on ice? What about sleighing and sliding down hill? What is the contrivance for making heavily-loaded carts go down steep hills safely? How does the steam make the locomotive go? What is the difference between the driving-wheels and the small wheels? What comparison is made about these two kinds of wheels? How do the driving-wheels move the locomotive along? What is said about the rails being too smooth? How is the difficulty remedied? How is it after the locomotive is well agoing when the rails are slippery? What is the comparison about running on the ice? How do brakes operate in stopping the cars? What else is done when they want to stop the cars quickly? What is said about greasing and oiling wheels? What is said about the joints of machinery and the joints of our bodies? What is said about the friction of water on rocks? What about the friction of air? What is true of all motion on the earth? What is said about the earth as it goes around the sun?

CHAPTER XXXV.
CONCLUSION.

I HAVE thus, in the Three Parts of this book, described to you some of the wonderful things that are all around you upon the earth and in the water. But there are many more things than I have described. In this book you have only begun to learn what is in the world, and you could not learn all if you should study all your lifetime, and even if your life should be as long as Methuselah's was. But I hope that you will go on to learn as much as you can. With your mind wide awake, you will see and hear, as you go about from day to day, a great many interesting things that I have not mentioned. I have told you about many things in plants; but if you look at different plants as you meet with them, you will soon see that you can learn much about them that you can not find any where in this book. So, also, if you watch animals, large and small, as you see them, you will find many more interesting things in them than I have told you. And the same is true of the subjects of the Third Part—air, water, light, etc. I have only opened to you a few of the leaves in the Book of Nature, and you can go on to open more of them for yourselves.

To know much about things, you must not merely look at them. You must examine them—that is, you must think while you look. You must think what this is for and what that is for. In this way you can find out a great deal for yourselves. You will not merely see that what I and others tell you is true, but you will find out things that no one has told you, and perhaps some things that no one has found out before you. Newton, who found out so many things that men did not before know, always thought about things as he saw them; and so did Franklin, who, as you remember, discovered that lightning is electricity. They began early, when they were children, to think while they looked. They had a *habit* of doing it. If they had not, they would not have been such discoverers. Though perhaps none of you may ever discover as many things or as great things as they did, any of you may make some discoveries. Though your discoveries may be small ones, they are not to be despised. They will be worth something. *Every fact that is found out is of some value.* And if you always think while you see and hear, you may find out for yourselves many facts, and some of them may prove to be of great value.

Sometimes a fact that would appear to be of no value turns out to be worth a great deal. Most people would not think that there was much to be learned from a hen's muddy tracks on a pile of sugar; but, as you remember I told you in Part First, Chapter XXIX., some one observed the fact that the sugar was whitened wherever the tracks were, and thought about this fact; and the result was that moistened clay came to be used in every sugar refinery in whitening sugar.

One that is in the habit of thinking while he looks will find something interesting wherever he goes. He will not be obliged to go to some museum to see wonderful things, but he will find them all about him. In the most common plants and animals, which most people do not think of much, he will see many things to interest and astonish him; and to him the air and the water, and even the stones under his feet, will be full of wonders.

You see by what I have said that there is a great deal to

be learned that is not in books. Indeed, books will not do you much good if they do not wake up in you a disposition to learn more than they tell you. People that know much are not content with learning merely what they find in books, but learn what they can from every body and from every thing. They use books only as helps, and the most of what they know they learn by observing—that is, seeing and thinking upon what they see.

It is very pleasant to know the reasons of things. I have therefore told you in this book, as I have gone along, as much as I could do, why things are as I have described them; but you will remember that I have now and then said about some things that you are not old enough yet to understand them. As you grow older you can learn more and more, and so the things that you will be interested in will be all the time increasing. But, though you may keep on learning all your lives, there are some things that you never can understand. God understands the reasons of every thing, but there are many, very many things that the wisest of men can not explain.

Very wise men are not apt to be proud of their wisdom. They commonly feel that what they know is very little when it is compared with what they do not know. Newton was one of the wisest men that ever lived. He was so wise that he discovered more things than any other man ever has. But he was very humble about his knowledge. He said this about it: He felt that what he knew was like a few pebbles that he had picked up on the sea-shore, and that there was so much of what he did not know that it was like the great ocean that was before him.

You remember that I told you in Part Second that all that we know we learn by the senses of our bodies—the sight, the hearing, etc. But the glorified bodies which the Bible says that we shall have in another life will be fitted with better means of getting knowledge. Some things that are mysterious to us now we shall then understand. We shall know more than Newton and all the wise men of this world ever knew here, and we shall ever be learning more and more of the wonders of God's power, and wisdom, and goodness.

Questions.—*What* is said about learning all that is in the world? How can you learn about things for yourselves? What is said about Newton and Franklin? Can you make some discoveries? What is said about the value of facts? What about finding wonders all around us? How can books help you to learn more than is in them? What is said about understanding the reasons of things? What is said about the feelings of very wise men? Tell what Newton said about his knowledge. What is said about our getting knowledge in another world?

THE END.